WAKEFUL CHILDREN

WAKEFUL CHILDREN

A Collection of Horror and Supernatural Tales

Best Wishes,

S P Oldham

S. P. OLDHAM

Matador
9 Priory Business Park,
Wistow Road, Kibworth Beauchamp,
Leicestershire. LE8 0RX
Tel: 0116 279 2299
Email: books@troubador.co.uk
Web: www.troubador.co.uk/matador
Twitter: @matadorbooks

ISBN: 978 1789010 145

British Library Cataloguing in Publication Data.
A catalogue record for this book is available from the British Library.

Printed and bound in Great Britain by 4edge Limited
Typeset in 11pt Minion Pro by Troubador Publishing Ltd, Leicester, UK

Matador is an imprint of Troubador Publishing Ltd

To my family, with love and gratitude for your eternal support.

Also in memory of my father,
James Albert Mitchell
whose horror books I used to sneak from his shelves when I thought
he wasn't looking and to whom I owe my love of the genre.

Dad, I think you might have liked this…

S P Oldham

CONTENTS

JOE GALLOWS

His real name was lost to all memory, his own included; the locals called him Joe Gallows. He had no idea where the 'Joe' came from; the 'Gallows' he understood absolutely.

He had a need for a very particular kind of slaughter. Using a slingshot, Gallows hunted down small prey; over time variously killing foxes, weasel, stoat, rats, birds and even once a small, crippled badger. He was careful only to stun them at first. When they began to show signs of recovery he would pull tighter on the noose he had slipped around their necks. It fascinated him, the way their eyes showed at first confusion, quickly becoming fear, then sheer panic before the light inside them slowly faded, extinguished into nothing more than sightless, glossy mirrors reflecting his image.

The next part was the real thrill; stringing them up,

three, four, even ten at a time, like macabre tinsel, from tree to tree, post to post, for the world to admire his skill.

He had started small, draping a string of corpses across a road sign, only to find it impossible to gauge people's reactions as they sped by in their cars. For all he knew they had not even spotted his work. One day, he dared to venture further into the village.

Little more than two streets in he had come across a section of security fencing around a house extension in progress; perfect. Better still, there was a defunct bus shelter just across the road.

Gallows reached into his back-pack and pulled out a loop of pre-strung animals, tying their shared noose into the security fence and fastening it securely. He spared only the briefest moment to admire his handiwork before retreating to a spot behind the shelter.

At last, as he had anticipated, the front door to the house opened. Two teenage girls emerged, picking their way carefully around stacks of paving slabs and rows of glossy new piping. They were so preoccupied with buttoning up coats against the chill that it took an age before one of them finally looked up.

The girl stopped fiddling with her coat and Gallows heard her breathe, "Tasha, what the hell is that?"

Tasha shrugged off-handedly, "What's what Mel?"

"That!" Mel hissed, pointing at the fence.

Tasha peered, "I don't know," she said, "Let's go a bit closer."

"I don't think I want to. I think we should go in and get dad."

"To tell him what? That there's something on the fence, we don't know what, but could he get up early on his one day off and come and look because we're too scared to?"

"Okay, let's get mum then,"

"Don't be such a baby! It's just some old rags or something. Come on," she urged, "we'll look together."

It had only taken a few more steps. Tasha was the first to comprehend what she was looking at. Her hand flew to her mouth and she gagged as if about to vomit. Mel stopped dead in her tracks and even from his hiding place, Gallows could see her complexion pale suddenly. She emitted a small shriek, like a muted scream, apparently unable either to move or to tear her gaze away from the communal hanging on the fence before her. Tasha was also the first to recover; she began running, pulling her shocked sister awkwardly along behind her, both of them stumbling and tripping in their haste to escape the sight.

Gallows stood up arthritically slowly, rubbing his back and shuffling out into the road as if he was merely a tramp waking stiffly to another cold day. He paused long enough to see the front door open to the girls' frenzied pounding. He couldn't have asked for a better response.

He fed off the memory of that morning for days. The urge to repeat it became irresistible. He redoubled his efforts, his work becoming infamous locally. Village wide, people were finding strings of slaughtered animals adorning walls, hedgerows, gates; anywhere Gallows deemed worthy of his attentions.

He thought he had planned his decoration of the school well.

This was the riskiest one yet; he just hoped the rewards would be worth it. Checking he was unobserved as best he could, Gallows broke cover from the neat row of trees that lined the car park to loop the readily prepared line of cold, dead animals along the railings.

The fence was higher than he had reckoned with and he spent a few moments straining to reach the top in order to hang his trophies. Feeling the thrilling pressure of time, he finally succeeded and stepped back briefly to survey his work.

This was a row of stiff little bodies; tiny paws and tails rigid in death. Gallows stuffed the now empty sack into the folds of his coat and made for the cover of the trees once again. He had an escape route onto the street, the broken wire fence behind him held down with rocks to allow for a quick escape. Confident, excitement mounting, he waited.

He heard approaching voices; a cacophony of 'hellos' and snippets of mundane conversation as children and parents approached the school grounds. He relished the familiar dark frisson of thrill when he heard the first exclamations of horror.

On the pathway a man began waving his arms wildly, shouting for everyone to stop, to go back, but for some school-goers it was too late. Several children began to cry, though Gallows noted with satisfaction that others seemed more curious than upset.

The man had stopped waving and had moved to stand in front of the hangings, attempting to block them from view with outstretched arms. Someone else ran into the school building to alert the powers within.

Barely a minute later, a bespectacled man in an expensive looking suit came hurrying out, his face pale with concern. A second man clad in khaki overalls ran alongside him. He was pulling on rubber gloves and carrying a thick black bag, his expression grim. It was obvious these two intended to take his trophies down. Gallows had seen enough; he turned to leave.

Two men waited for him as he stepped out onto the street behind the pinned down fencing. Their expressions were mixtures of contempt and hostility. There was a large woman with them, her weathered face contorted with disgust, meaty arms folded across her ample chest. Her voice trembled as she spoke, "You low-life piece of shit! How dare you? How dare you do something like that in a school? A fucking school?"

Gallows grimaced, for once caught unawares.

"Don't you smile at me," The woman took a step closer, her fists clenched.

One of the men caught her elbow, "Leave off Debs, I want a word with him." He pulled Debs aside and seized Gallows by his tattered jacket, slamming him hard against a parked car. He leaned in to deliver a threat, then reeled back, repulsed by Gallows' putrid breath.

"Jesus Christ! He stinks!" He heaved and retched violently.

"He probably eats road-kill," the other man eyed Gallows contemptuously; "You ever eat your road kill weirdo?"

The man holding Gallows recovered, wiping his mouth on his sleeve, being careful now to keep Gallows at arm's length, "You won't do this shit around here anymore, will you Joe Gallows? Oh yeah, we all know it's you leaving your sorry little calling cards all over the place."

Despite his discomfort at such close human contact, Gallows felt a swell of pride at the recognition. He made a wet, purring noise deep in his throat. Immediately wary, the man's grip tightened.

"Don't even fucking think about spitting on me. I'll give you such a kicking, there won't be enough of you left to hang up anywhere, you understand me?" He stared into Gallows' amber eyes intending to force his point home, but was immediately caught by the strange light he saw there. It held him bound and for a moment he almost forgot his purpose. He looked down at the ragged coat still bunched in his own fists as if surprised to find he was gripping it.

Gallows stared mutely back, an ooze of saliva tracing its slow way down his stubbly chin. Sickened and seemingly imbued with fresh anger, the man pulled Gallows in close and then shoved him away hard.

Gallows smashed against the parked car, twisting mid fall. His face hit the front tyre, sending blunt shafts of pain into his forehead and leaving a tarry black smudge across the bridge of his nose. The road beneath was unforgiving; small, stinging shards of gravel embedded themselves spitefully into his palms and his knees throbbed with pain, yet he did not attempt to rise until his tormentors had moved off.

They appeared oddly subdued as they went, the man who had shoved him pushing his hands deep into his pockets, Debs arms folded about herself as if seeking reassurance. She turned to look back once, hurrying onwards as fast as her ample frame could carry her when she saw Gallows was watching.

Gallows had forgotten the second man; he didn't see the kick to his stomach coming as he finally tried to stand. The blow drove the air from his lungs, winding him. Waves of agony rippled the length of his body, rendering him paralysed. A second kick followed, pitching him heavily forwards. He saw his precious slingshot tumble from his pocket and skitter away. He saw it snapped beneath the deliberate weight of his attacker.

Then his forehead connected with the road too, becoming as pitted with stones as his hands were; it felt like a thousand rodent teeth trying to burrow into his brain.

His eyes were streaming, his kidneys aching beyond comprehension, his stomach cramping. It felt like an eternity that he lay wedged between the kerb and the car, willing the white waves of agony to end.

They subsided at last, allowing him to sit cautiously back on his knees; he could tolerate the pain now, but the damage to his sling-shot was devastating; snapped in two places and dangling like a broken limb from a stretched and useless tendon when he crawled over to it and picked it up.

Gallows moaned; the grief of this loss worse than the physical pain. It didn't matter that he could always make another. This was *his*; his belonging, his possession; the man might as well have stolen it from him.

He was fighting this keen wave of loss when a strange

new sensation overcame him. A wetness began to spread over his back; a shower of warm liquid spattering him from above, speckling his filthy coat. Confused, Gallows tried to work out where it was coming from.

There was a small, strident sound as the man zipped up his jeans, "Piss on you, sicko!" He sneered, swaggering away, his demeanour defiant, nothing lost of his earlier aggression.

Still cradling the broken catapult as if he might somehow bring it back to life, Gallows stayed where he was in the gutter and watched him go.

Over the ensuing weeks, Gallows made it his mission to find out where that man's home was. He understood better than anyone the need to inflict pain; he knew better than most the relief of violence, but what this man had done to him was inexcusable. The lowest form of behaviour; not even dogs pissed on each other. He could have forgiven him the kicking, but the abuse and the broken catapult meant the man had gone too far. Now Gallows had to make things right.

When he finally discovered where he lived, the delicious turnings of fate made him shiver with anticipation. It was the security fence house, the extension now complete, the building materials all gone to be replaced by an open and inviting new driveway.

The man had accosted him on the street behind the primary school, but Gallows knew from his first visit to the house that the girls that lived there were in their teens. There must be another, younger child then; why else would he have been at the school? Once more sheltering behind the bus stop across the road, Gallows laid low.

His patience was rewarded when the man came strolling from the garden onto his driveway. He watched as he pulled a set of car keys out of his pockets, climbed into his battered old transit van, a name stencilled in large print across its side panels, and drove off.

Gallows could read, though his use for the skill was minimal. The last time he read willingly was when he found a discarded local paper with a photo of his animal bunting in it. Amazed, he had torn the picture and its caption out. He had read it so many times now he knew it by heart; *'Evidence of a Sick Mind at Work or a Cry for Help from a Desperate Man?'* He was not sure what it meant, but he could read it well enough; just as he could read what was on that van.

'T.J. Russell,' it read, below which were three pictures, each underscored by a word; *'Windows, Doors, Conservatories.'* There was a phone number which Gallows did not bother to read; he had no use for numbers.

Encouraged, he watched on. Just as before, the girls left for school, chattering and unaware. Not much later a delicate looking boy of about seven or eight stepped out of the house, the same woman who had opened the door that first morning following close behind him. Gallows waited until they reached the end of the road and were out of sight before crossing.

He peered in at the windows to make sure the house

was empty. There was no obvious sign of occupation, so he moved around to the side gate. It was closed but unlocked.

He tensed; no dog came snarling and growling. Warily he turned into the garden; nothing there but a small patch of lawn, a rotary washing line and a set of patio furniture complete with canopied swing chair. Sitting improbably on top of it, eyeing him with lazy curiosity, was a fat tabby cat.

The cat eyed Gallows with disdain. Tail twitching, it tolerated his approach until he reached up to stroke it. The cat hissed violently, streaking a claw neatly across Gallows face before leaping down and slinking away.

Gallows shrieked girlishly; razor-like incisions crossed across his face, slicing into the white of his left eye and the soft flesh of his nostrils. He fell to his knees, rocking in agony. When the worst of it subsided, he peered about him, his eye already beginning to swell. The cat had curled up snugly on one of the patio chairs, no longer remotely concerned.

As always, Gallows back-pack was tucked beneath his clothing. He pulled it out, took out his newly made slingshot and loaded it with a steel nut. He took careful aim, ignoring his bleeding eye, intent only on the small, soft skull of the cat.

It was a good shot, despite his new handicap. There was a wet pop, like a cork reluctantly leaving a bottle. The cat's body went rigid for an instant, then relaxed back into almost the same cosy position it had been lying in. There was no blood, just an obviously fatal dent. The top of the delicate head had caved inwards. Gallows fingered the spot;

fragments of jagged bone grated against one another as he pushed deeper, reaching a spongier texture he guessed was the brain. Deprived of the pleasure of strangulation he withdrew his finger and picked the cat up.

He took a ball of twine from his pack, looped it around the cat's neck and pegged it up on the rotary line. He set it spinning, the cat's body jerking a peg loose to leave it dangling at a strange angle.

The pain in his eye ebbed and flowed and had begun to itch infuriatingly. Scratching at it furiously, Gallows sought refuge behind the shed, taking time to lock the gate first.

The day passed slowly. Gallows eye felt like a rock in his head; heavy and hard. His other eye had begun to itch too, making him panic; losing his sight, however temporarily, would ruin his plans. He spent the day behind the shed alternately rocking in pain and weeping silently into his hands, craving release from the agony. The first glimmer that there might yet be some relief came when he heard childish voices behind the gate,

They were arguing. Gallows froze, listening.

"Well I don't know why it's locked, do I?" Tasha was saying, "Maybe dad locked it,"

"But he never locks it! He knows we need to get in after school"

"Look Mel, don't blame me, I didn't lock the damn thing!"

"So what are we going to do?" This was the boy, his voice softer than that of his bigger sisters, "Just wait around here?"

"No Gabriel, we are not going to just wait around here at all! Someone has to climb the gate and unlock it, that's all," There was a pause. If Tasha had been waiting for her siblings to volunteer she was to be disappointed, "Oh for god's sake! I'll do it,"

Gallows watched as Mel's head rose over the gate. She sat awkwardly atop it for a second, then swung her leg over and dropped to the ground with a graceless thud.

The gate open, Gabriel ducked between his sisters and went straight to a drainpipe running vertically down the back wall. He stuck his hand inside and pulled out a length of wire with a small plastic wallet attached. Taking out a key he unlocked the side door. Gallows, squinting and sweating, watched them go inside, listening for the tumblers to click back into place as they locked the door behind them. They didn't.

He let some time pass before following.

The door opened into an area housing washing machines on one side, a rack of coat hooks and shoe shelves on the other. Before he could reach to open a second door immediately in front of him it flew open and Gabriel burst in, shouting *shut up* over his shoulder as Mel called him from somewhere beyond.

Gallows' reaction was instinctive. His hand flashed out, catching the boy by the throat. He kicked the door shut and pinned the flailing child up against it. Caught utterly by surprise, Gabriel tried to kick out, but it was useless. Gallows had pinned a knee across the child's skinny legs and increased the pressure on his neck. He watched fascinated as the eyes began to bulge, the tiny capillary veins popping inside. He felt something snap under the pressure of his thumb and the child grew rapidly weaker. His last, involuntary act was to empty his bladder, soaking Gallows shoes.

Gallows was disgusted; the child had abused him just as his father had done. He almost allowed his rage to get the better of him, nearly hurling the lifeless form across the small space to smash against the wall. The rage passed and as he always did in the end, Gallows chose instead to hang him contemptuously from the coat hooks, looping his school shirt over a peg to let his small frame droop forwards like a puppet that had had its strings cut.

Wiping his shoes as best he could on one of the coats, Gallows turned back to the door. A slice of pain seared into his forehead as his eye began a new attack. Groaning, he leant against the frame to steady himself.

The door led into a newly fitted kitchen which in turn led into a large hallway. There were strains of music coming from upstairs, competing with the noise of a television blaring from somewhere to his left. His jaw beginning to ache now too, Gallows climbed the stairs.

He reached the top unchallenged, where he paused to pinpoint the direction the music was coming from. The monotonous beat led him to a door left slightly ajar down the landing, allowing him to see in.

Tasha was lying on her bed, her back to him. Gallows slinked into the room. He had intended using his bare hands but there was a set of earphones left untidily on the bedside table, the lead dangling to the floor. Suppressing a groan, Gallows bent to pick it up.

The room reverberating to the music, his injured eye seemed to pulse in time. Gallows knew his next move had to be quick. He leaned over the bed, anticipating that she would sense his presence any moment now. He was right; Tasha pushed herself up on one elbow, turning to see who was behind her. It was all Gallows needed.

He slipped the wire over her head and pulled it back into her neck in one fluid movement. Surprised, the girl struggled to get to her knees, clutching at the cord, already struggling to draw enough breath to scream. Gallows, his body supporting her from behind, pulled the unforgiving lead harder still.

The ferocity of her desperation was intense, but brief. She struggled to claw at Gallows' swollen face, missing and gouging a long nail deep into his ear lobe. Sweating profusely now he ignored it, increasing the pressure. She scrabbled at the wire at her throat. Unable to grip it she scratched at it madly; her sharp, brightly coloured nails raking her own skin, catching her lips and tearing those too, her panic increasing.

Gallows pulled the wire tighter, cutting deep. At last the skin ruptured, leaving the wire edged with a sticky rime of blood. The salty tang of their combined sweat was at once overwhelmed by another, more powerful stench as her bowels gave way, staining her jeans a hot, wet brown against Gallows knee. All at once it was over; her bloodied hands, the nails torn and mangled, fell dead into her lap as if she was conceding defeat. Gallows relaxed the tension on the wire and her head lolled heavily, tearing the gash wider, the wire jutting from it like a thin second tongue.

Her own was purple and grotesque, sticking out between her ragged lips as if in mimicry.

Relaxing, Gallows loosened his grip and assessed the situation. Tasha's badly ravaged neck meant changing his plans for her; there was no question of hanging her by it now.

Besides, she had abused him in an even more foul fashion than her animal brother and father had, the stinking evidence of it now cooling on his knee; she was deserving of a greater punishment.

He pulled the plug on the stereo. The blaring music had been a cover for his attack, but he needed quiet now; had Mel heard something downstairs and was running to see what was wrong? He stood out on the landing, slingshot ready; nothing. Chances were she hadn't heard over the din from the T.V.

Content, Gallows went back into the bedroom, rummaging in the folds of his reeking clothing for a coil of thin rope. He knelt at Tasha's feet and wound it round her ankles, binding them tightly, being sure to leave a length free. Then he carried her out to the banisters, cradling her almost gently in his arms, a trail of blood and excrement dotting their progress.

He reached the banister and set Tasha down close to it. Working quickly now, he used the spare length of rope to tie her bound ankles to a spindle, tugging hard to ensure it would hold. Risking that it would take her dead weight, he hoisted her over the top and let go.

The rope was too short: her feet had come to a stop about halfway down the banisters. She was facing the floor at an unnatural angle, her ripped neck tearing further. Clots of fresh gore hit the clean tiles below like bloody water bombs. Excrement mingled with it, lacing its way down her back, threading through her hair and spotting brown amongst the deep red like modern art.

Perhaps the stench had penetrated the wall of sound. The volume of the television was muted and from the lounge Mel called, "Tasha what's that noise? You okay?"

Gallows held the slingshot ready. Mel called out again, "Tasha?" Then, as he had known she would, she stepped into the soiled hallway, her face a picture of pale uncertainty.

He didn't give her time to fully take in the scene before her. His eye was so swollen now he needed time to get in a second shot should he need it. His aim was still good; the bolt found its mark dead centre of Mel's forehead. The colour flooded from her; she dropped where she stood, falling against the telephone table to bring it crashing down, a cup of pens smashing and scattering everywhere.

Gallows shoved the slingshot back into his pockets as he descended the stairs. Reaching Mel, he grabbed her by the hair and pulled her across the floor, smearing her through the foul drippings of her dead sister. He almost slipped once, his feet skating beneath him as if on ice, making him reach out to the wall for support. He righted himself, oblivious to the slingshot as it fell.

He dragged Mel through the glossy kitchen, bumping her roughly down the step into the utility room past the drooping Gabriel. The boy's shirt had torn on the hook, leaving him bent over as if examining his shoes. Gallows paid him no attention as he once more opened the outer door.

There was no sign of movement outside, no cars pulling into the drive out front. He dragged Mel ruthlessly over the threshold, grazing the soft skin of her back and thighs. He dragged her past the stiffening cat to the high panel fencing at the end of the garden. There he wound twine around Mel's neck several times, shouldered her weight and grunting with effort, propped her into an almost standing position.

She murmured softly, an unintelligible sound that told him she was still alive. Excited at the thought, Gallows looped the other end of twine around the top of the fence post and pulled.

Mel's eyes snapped open as if the action had jolted her awake. Her forehead was mottled in shades of purple and blue, the bruising from the bolt already evident. The slow strangulation Gallows now applied made those shades more vivid still.

Mel had no fight left in her. It was easy for Gallows to wrap the other end of twine tightly around his own wrists. When it was done, the twine cutting into his wrists, he raised his knees and swung, his entire body weight acting as a pulley, raising Mel higher, pulling her noose far tighter. He dangled there for as long as he could, like a child on a garden swing. Then he left her hanging like a limp scarecrow, feet barely three inches from the ground. He fled as fast as he was able, slamming the gate so hard behind him that it flew open again, an invitation to anyone to come inside and look around.

He barely escaped; even now the white van was rounding the bend at the end of the street. He heard the van doors sliding open and slamming shut. He heard Russell's voice, deep and assured and the lighter tones of his wife. They would discover them together then; discover what it meant to abuse Joe Gallows.

It was too much to permeate Russell's mind. He recalled his wife screaming; *screaming*. He was dimly aware of people around them, though he had no idea when they had arrived. Someone was vomiting on his front doorstep. The police had not yet arrived. Someone else said they were calling for an ambulance.

"What for?" Russell had asked, "They are all dead."

He went from Mel to Gabe to poor, violated Tasha; hopelessly revisiting their deaths, knowing there was nothing he could do. He wanted to drop to his knees at Tasha's feet and beg forgiveness, but he could not bring himself to kneel amongst her bodily fluids, feeling it a desecration; she had been soiled enough. He bent his head instead, awash with despair; that was when he saw it.

The slingshot was resting innocently against the skirting board. Russell reached out and picked it up in disbelief. He stared at it for what felt like an age before he looked up at his wife; did she know what it meant? Did she understand?

She was beside herself, blind with grief and sobbing hopelessly, half collapsed in the arms of a neighbour who was shakily trying to lead her away from the horror. There was no way of assuaging her grief any more than there was a way to assuage his own; but this slingshot was all he needed to give him reason for vengeance. Russell could do that much. His wife was safer in the care of their neighbours; for he had never felt such a desolate rage as the one that consumed him now.

He went out to his van, shouldering aside all attempts to stop him. He dimly heard an entreaty to stay with his wife, that she needed him. Someone, a man, grabbed his shoulder as he climbed into the cab, warning him to stay calm, to see reason, to wait for the police; Russell brushed him off as if he wasn't there.

Everyone knew Gallows haunted the woods.

He turned the key in the ignition and pulled out onto the cold, surreal street.

Gallows' heart was pounding. It had all gone so well, the only thing to spoil it that damned cat. His eyes felt huge; tight and full of fluid, the grotesquely enlarged eyelids pressuring the tender eyeballs beneath. The bridge of his nose had also begun to swell and itch maddeningly. There was an intense tingling, burning sensation at the back of his throat and his tongue felt thick and furry. He longed to stop and vomit, but he dared not slow down until he had reached the safety of his woods.

He stumbled into the welcoming fringe of conifers just as the unmistakable sound of an engine reached him from the road. Ducking low, Gallows hoped it would pass him by as so many cars had done before. Not this time. The van stopped a few yards from where he crouched, the headlights washing over him. Too dangerous to stay here, Gallows had no choice but to break cover and run.

The movement caught Russell's eye the minute Gallows made it. The man was fast, like some woodland creature. Russell had barely set off to catch him before Gallows melted into the treeline.

"*Gallows!*" Russell screamed into the woods, "Gallows you fucking low-life! Where are you? Where are you, you fucking baby-killer!" Russell's voice faltered, becoming a choked sob. "I'm coming for you; do you hear me? I'm coming and oh God I am going to do so much more than piss on you now. *So* much more."

Gallows was appalled at the heaviness of his own legs and at how quickly he had lost momentum. He knew there was a hiding place close by if he could just find the strength to get to it.

Russell was still shouting, "I found your slingshot, you vermin! I found it and I am going to find some interesting new ways to use it when I get my hands on you, you lousy, filthy, stinking bastard!"

Gallows throat was threatening to close up. His struggle to breathe was becoming harder and what little he could draw he was exhaling in a high, whistling wheeze, the sound such a dead giveaway he might as well have stood in the glare of Russell's headlights with his hands up.

Russell heard it clearly; he cocked his ear to listen again. Gallows tried to contain it, but it was beyond his control. Another desperate, sucking gasp and again the whistling sound followed. Gallows chest hurt, his ribs were sore to touch. What the hell was the matter with him? He'd been fine until that damned cat had sliced its claws across his face.

In direct mimicry of so many of his victims, he scrabbled at his throat as if to pull away a noose that was not there. He crouched, all else forgotten as he battled for the most fundamental of all needs; to breathe.

Russell's booted feet entered Gallows limited pool of sight. He expected a kick to the stomach or a fist to the head, half wishing the man would get on with it and put him out of his misery, but no blows came.

"Yours, I think," Russell tossed the slingshot contemptuously at the stricken Gallows, who even in his need to draw air, reached out for it compulsively, clinging it to him like a child might a comfort toy. Russell sneered derisively.

"Well what the fuck happened to you? Someone get to you before I did?" He was panting hard too, his voice shaking with emotion. "One of my kids," here his voice broke and he had to gather himself before he could go on, "one of my kids fight back? Was it Tasha? She's a feisty little thing, my Tasha. Was it her? *Was it her?*" The last question was roared into Gallows' ear adding a strange, piercing pain to the cacophony of agony already in his head.

"Caad," Gallows gargled the sound, "Caad." He continued to claw at his neck pathetically, bloodying it still further.

Russell's stomach was churning, waiting for Gallows to say one word, just one word, about his precious kids because then he knew he would be able finally to lose all reason and pound the bastard to death, leaving his slingshot rammed down his throat for good measure. "What? What the fuck are you saying? Are you saying my babies' names? Are you trying to tell me about my poor, dead babies? *Are you?*"

"Caad," Gallows slurred, his mouth filling with froth, bubbling grey-white out of the corner of his mouth, "c-a-d."

"*Cad?* C-a-d? Cat? You mean *cat?* The cat did this to you? Mr. Sphinx?"

Gallows slumped onto his side, the rise and fall of his chest becoming more shallow and infrequent. Russell gave a harsh, disbelieving laugh, "You're allergic to cats! Wonder if you ever knew that? I mean cats were not your normal prey, were they? Were kids? Huh? Were kids your normal prey?"

Russell hefted Gallows up, leaning him awkwardly against a tree trunk, reminding him of his poor, poor Mel, lolling against the fence in the garden. It robbed him of his strength momentarily. All he could do was whisper in Gallows ear, pushing aside the stink of the man, to say, "Funny, isn't it? All the small, wild creatures you tortured and killed over the years, and now you're finished by a fucking house cat!"

Gallows was wheezing madly, whistling high. His stupid, filthy being was suddenly too much for Russell.

He loosed a punch at Gallows' misshapen features, his

fist catching the swelling mass. It made a sickly sound as it burst open, yellow pus flowering at the impact. Gallows tried to scream with the blistering pain but he had no breath left to do it. Russell felt his gorge rise in revulsion. He turned away, retching, everything suddenly pointless and repulsive.

Gallows gurgled and frothed, far beyond speech now.

Wiping spittle from his mouth, Russell watched him die, a strange detachment settling over him. There was no death rattle like they show in all the movies; Gallows did not have enough of a face left to form any sort of recognisable sound. It was more a bubbling, oozing, sucking mess. There was one final feeble, wet noise and then nothing more; no movement, no sound, just a heavy stillness.

The same stillness fell upon Russell, as if Gallow's death was catching. He was not aware of time passing, though at some point he understood there were sirens approaching. Flashing blue lights sent crazily bright circles around the darkened woods, flushing out its most secret corners. All at once the area became busy with the slamming of car doors, hurrying uniforms, the buzz of radio contact; he could almost hear the guard of professional procedure being slid into place as a defence against the real horror of the scene. He wished he could hide behind it himself. Instead he was immersed in it; stinking with it and he felt he could never be clean again.

Gallows neither saw nor heard any of it. There were no eyes with which to see; shrouded as they were beneath ripped and fetid folds of skin and the putrid mess they had held tight within. Nothing by which to measure a fading light; nothing to show a last reflection.

Soft voiced paramedics appeared from the ether, mouthing words that were meant to be comforting but which barely reached Russell as he allowed himself to be half led, half carried like an invalid to a waiting vehicle.

He cast a final glance at the wrecked form of Gallows as it was lifted into a body bag. It didn't register at once, the shock and leaching adrenalin preventing him from thinking clearly. It was only when he was safely ensconced in the back of a waiting police car that he thought to ask why the body bag hadn't been zipped up the whole way.

"You sure you want to know? You've been through enough already I would guess," the officer had cautioned.

"I want to know," Russell's voice was hoarse.

The officer nodded resignedly, "Well, it seems they couldn't get the zip up past his neck, it was so swollen. They were afraid too much pressure around that area might make it burst the way his face did,"

"Swollen?" Russell thought for a moment, "As if he had been, I don't know, hanged or strangled and left dangling or something?" *'The way my children were,'* he didn't say out loud.

The officer seemed to understand, "Maybe," he nodded thoughtfully, "maybe,"

The officer glanced in the mirror, checking on his passenger. He was surprised to find a smile playing on Russell's lips, though his eyes were raw with pain and shock. Russell caught him checking on him.

"It's ok officer," Russell reassured him, "I was just

thinking what a good cat Mr. Sphinx was. Or should I say 'caad?' Caad?"

Later they all ascribed it to shock, of course; but the officer would never quite forget how Russell laughed softly all the way to the station.

ABSORPTION

Silence hangs like a storm-cloud over the sleeping occupants of Oakwood Close, watched over by the very tree that gave the cul-de-sac its name.

There should be sound here; small creatures that chirrup, snuffle and rustle, busy about their nocturnal business, engaged in the blood-hungry drama of eat or be eaten that ensures life's continuance.

Look closer.

See the hedgehog on the lawn? It won't pause, but passes through as quickly as its stump legs will allow. Watch the fox, warily approaching the bins; his senses tell him there is something wrong here. The carcass of a chicken in an open bin is not temptation enough to stay; he turns and runs, unnerved.

Close your eyes and look deeper; use your inner eye. Watch the spiders; they never stray from their webs. See the woodlice in their armoured shells; the slugs, defenceless. Spy the beetles, shiny beneath the shelter of the wooden shed.

Go deeper still; let your vision sink into the damp soil. What do we have here? Earthworms, industrious and ignorant; perhaps a mole, labouring in blind panic against the darkness.

There is something else here.

An ancient, heavy stench fills your nostrils, older than the soil itself. You sense something; some force seeking, searching for the very centre of the world it seems. It is inexorable, unstoppable; you know this.

You follow, deeper still; beyond the foundations of the houses' steel and concrete roots. It is close now; you can feel the dull, slow thump of some life force. Terrified, you want both to see it and to turn away.

Mud and clay begin to fill your ears, block your nostrils. You try to scream and the taste of earth, organic, metallic, clogs your throat. Soil grits your eyes and leaves them sore and grainy. You cough and choke; the weight of the earth is unbearable, breaking your back, crushing your lungs.

Come back. Come up again, to the world.

You went too close.

The oak sways gently, a shiver shimmers its way from roots to tip. A branch creaks as if in resistance.

A small, fresh leaf strains to curl into life, shows promise for an instant, then withers and dies. A sigh, just beyond human hearing, vibrates the night.

All else is still.

Number 8, Oakwood Close.

Ryan opened his eyes; he had hardly closed them all night anyway. The settee was too small for a grown man to sleep on comfortably. He sat up gingerly, rubbing his aching neck and yawning. Maybe Claire would be calmer now; maybe he could talk her round.

His stood and turned around. That's when he saw the cases. She'd never packed his bags before; threatened to many times, but never actually done it. When had Claire put them there?

He was amazed he hadn't heard her struggle down the stairs with them; he must have fallen asleep at some point after all.

He hesitated, unsure of his next move. After some anxious debate, he decided he would go up to her. He would find her warm and soft, sleepy in bed. A few well-chosen words, gentle hands, tender kisses…

The bedroom door was locked. Ryan knocked tentatively; no response. He tried again and then called her name, expecting to hear her familiar, half-awake murmur in reply.

"Your bags are packed. Get out,"

Claire sounded wide-awake and like she meant every word; her tone was final and flat. Ryan had never known her like this before.

"Claire babe, let me in. We need to talk,"

"There's nothing to talk about. I've heard all your lies before and I've got nothing to say to you. Get out,"

"Claire babe, please, just open the door,"

"It's better for you if I don't Ryan, believe me. Just go,"

"Better for me? What the hell's that supposed to mean?"

"Ryan, you're trying my patience,"

Flummoxed, Ryan gave up for a moment. He sat on the top stair, head in hands. It felt like he had a hangover, but he hadn't touched a drop last night. His head was sinning; a moment of sudden irrational anger flooded through him. He stood again, slamming his fists against the bedroom door, "To hell with this Claire! Open the door before I break it down!"

He heard her swear under her breath, then pad across to the door. The key turned in the lock. He turned the handle. Claire was sitting on the edge of the bed. Like him, she was still wearing the clothes she had on the night before; like him, she too was barefoot. She looked tired and worn. Ryan felt a rush of concern and affection for her. She looked small and fragile, sitting there.

He went to her, intending to cradle her; to kiss her tired, swollen eyes, stroke her hair. He bent to lift her chin and was caught by the shocking sting of her hand, small and hard against his cheek.

His surprise rendered him defenceless against her next blow. She struck from the other side this time; long nails dragging down his face, his neck, her rings leaving scratches and cut; tearing his lips, her blows frenzied and wild. Ryan caught her wrists and held her back, slamming her up against the wall, screaming at her to stop. She gasped and fell limp.

Ryan looked down into Claire's deep brown eyes, searching for any sign of emotion. Regret maybe; love hopefully. His own eyes were filling with tears.

She spat in his face.

Disgusted, Ryan stepped back, releasing his grip.

"I told you not to come in here," her tone was sneering.

Ryan could think of nothing to say. Too choked to speak, he simply left the room, letting the door click quietly shut behind him.

The suitcases were heavy as he loaded them into the car. He knew without doubt that there was nothing to stay for now; maybe they could have got over his sleeping around. Maybe they could even have got over the way Claire attacked him.

But Ryan knew he would never overcome what he had seen when he had searched Claire's eyes. He had looked for hope, redemption even. What he had found chilled him to the bone. Something so akin to madness he had been almost glad to go.

Upstairs, an enquiring branch brushed against Claire's window pane. She turned to it and smiled, licking Ryan's blood from her fingers.

In the depths below the house, an ancient, gnarled root stretched and moaned as if in pleasure, unheard by all but the earth itself. The sap in the old tree rose in release. A new

acorn, small and perfect, burst into creation, in defiance of
the natural order; whole and ready, full of promise.

Number 11, Oakwood Close.

Nancy was ready for them this time.

She shifted in her seat, dislodging a large tom-cat who stood in protest, threw her a withering look and jumped from her lap to the newspaper-strewn floor. Other cats littered about the room paused in their ablutions to observe goings-on, before losing interest and skulking away to hide behind boxes or mounds of black bin bags.

Some of these bags had been torn open by curious felines. Their entrails spilled upon the dirty floor; rubbish pooled like blood around a wound.

What remained visible of the walls showed a grey, sickly colour. The curtains were matted and filthy, hanging limply from the rails.

Nancy sat, huge and sweating, in the room's only seat; a ripped and tatty armchair, the foam showing through in patches like spongy bones. Her clothes, the same ones every day, were stained and repulsive. Her pale, sallow skin hung in folds around her chin, her arms, her ankles. Her eyes were dead blue pools; illuminating only at the thought of her precious cats. Cats; all Nancy cared about, all she lived for. Her house stood, rotten and rotting, food and carpets mouldering; stinking and unwashed. Her cats were the exception. In the morass that was her kitchen one space lay clear and, by Nancy's standards, clean. It was laid with fresh paper daily, for the litter tray, with bowls of food and water. Nancy was careful to keep these clean, regularly emptying the litter tray into an open box which usually stood next to the greasy cooker. It didn't matter to Nancy; why should anyone else care? She never had visitors anyway.

But she was expecting some today.

'*You have got fourteen days to clean this place up Nancy*' they had said, '*Fourteen days; that's your last warning. You have to get rid of some of these cats too, if you want to stay here. You've got far too many. If you clean up your act, maybe we'll let you keep one or two, but the rest have to go,*'

Nancy's vacant features didn't stir, but inside her, anger welled, huge and all consuming. The cats had to go, they had said; and that was when they had begun to disappear.

She hadn't laid eyes on Lulu or Rocky for days now. She knew they were dead; knew it in her bones. She knew who had killed them too.

Silas hadn't come back this morning, either. He was always such a stickler for his routine. She could expect to hear his demanding mewls at around seven thirty each morning, hungry after his night's adventures.

It was nearly 11.45 now; no sign of him.

Nancy wondered how they were killing her cats; the manner of their deaths. Cars probably, she decided. Nice, new, distant cars; keeping their hands clean.

She grunted, wishing they would hurry up and come. Her hand dropped to the box at the side of the chair, newly placed there just last night. The litter box; brimming with foul smelling cat excrement and urine soaked sand, a faded mug sitting atop it. Perhaps she should move it into its final position now, in readiness.

With much wheezing effort, Nancy pulled herself out of the chair. It had taken a lot of time to move the box this far last night. It would take more effort now, to move it to the front door.

Breathing hard, Nancy pushed and shoved the box with her feet, ruching the scattered newspapers at her feet; spilling some of its contents as it hit the door frame.

One last, great effort was required of her now and then she would be ready. Sweating profusely for her efforts, red-faced, her huge, heaving stomach threatening to split like one of her black bags, Nancy took the mug and filled it, dipping it into the putrid mess inside the box. She waited; it was nearly time.

Silas lay stretched along a branch of the oak, his glassy eyes unseeing. Cramped beneath him, a stubborn green bud had been trying to force its way past, toward the light. Unable to do so, it had instead begun to bore a small, insistent hole into Silas, seeing the cat's lifeless body as nothing more than another organic layer off which to feed.

Below, a car pulled up outside number eleven, disgorging two men dressed in suits and a smartly attired woman holding a clip-board. The trio conferred for a moment on the pavement, then approached Nancy's front door, the woman knocking peremptorily.

Nancy gripped the cup; she was ready for them this time.

Number 13, Oakwood Close

The sun was high in the sky. Lucy wasn't quite big enough yet to reach the lock on the front door. More than anything, she wanted to go out into the sunshine and feel the breeze upon her skin. She wanted it even more than she wanted something to eat.

The house was dim, all its curtains drawn. Lucy had managed to pull the blinds open a little way in a downstairs room, but there was nothing to see out back. There was no-one to talk to; no one to complain to of her hunger and her loneliness. As young as she was, Lucy couldn't name the ache that always seemed to be part of her.

The fridge, standing open in the kitchen, was largely empty now. Lucy had eaten what she liked at first, leaving less appealing things until she was desperate. She had discovered that eggs straight from the shell didn't taste nice, and that some of the food that went all fuzzy and blue didn't taste too good either.

There were tins in the cupboard, but Lucy couldn't open them. She had cut herself trying once and the wound was still sore. An angry red, it had started to become tinged with green; the throbbing had kept her awake most of last night. She never slept well anyway, curled up under her bed; her favourite hiding place when she was afraid mummy might come looking again.

Mummy frightened Lucy when she was all crazy. She had seen people on television like that sometimes; their voices got strange and they couldn't stand up straight. Sometimes, just like them, mummy got angry for nothing. She would shout and throw things and smack Lucy hard, saying everything was all Lucy's fault. That's how Lucy knew herself to be a bad person.

Mummy would even say she hated Lucy; that she should have called her Lucifer.

Lucy had fallen asleep wondering what she meant, many a night.

Then mummy would drink some more, and Lucy would hide somewhere small and dark, like under her bed, and wait for her to fall asleep.

The next day was always the best; mummy would be tired and a little bit cross at first, but later she would invite Lucy to cuddle up in bed with her. She would kiss her and hold her tight and say she was sorry; that she didn't mean the things she said. That everything would be all right. Maybe they would fall asleep together, all warm and close. Sometimes mummy would go downstairs and fetch something for Lucy to eat; a packet of crisps perhaps, or some biscuits.

Those special moments never lasted long. Mummy would get her headaches again and Lucy knew the only thing to help her get better was one of those cold cans from the fridge.

Lucy hoped that today was the day the man would come in his van and bring some shopping. It was usually cans, but sometimes there would be other things in the crate; maybe something to eat.

Lucy looked forward to the man in the van coming to the house. She was always hopeful of him bringing something nice. She saw the way he gave her funny looks, but he never said anything to her. He never spoke much at all; Lucy thought he always seemed in a big hurry.

Mummy might wake up and open the door, if he came. Otherwise, how would he get in?

Lucy's childish mind thought instantly of climbing. She would climb to open the front door.

Her eyes came to rest on one of the tall chairs around the table. They looked heavy; she would try to drag one to the door.

Hampered by her dirty nightdress catching on her small, cold feet, Lucy had trouble enough just dragging the chair away from the table. With a combination of desperation and excitement, she managed to wrestle the chair across the room and into the front hallway. She pushed it up against the door, hitched up her nightdress and clambered up.

The lock was tricky, Lucy had to struggle with the safety chain, but eventually she succeeded; the door was open!

She climbed down, feeling very pleased with herself. She pushed the heavy chair out of the way and pulled the door open.

The sun fell on her upturned face and warmed her through. The breeze blew in her unkempt hair and Lucy felt something so great, she had no words for it; a moment of sheer happiness. She squealed in delight and ran inside to tell mummy. If she would just come downstairs; just come and feel the sun…

She scampered up the stairs and into the gloomy bedroom. Lucy had become accustomed to the smell; it was old and stale, the smell Lucy always associated with mummy.

The floor was littered with empty cans. An empty bottle lay next to the bed, its neck shattered. Lucy was careful to go round the other side and avoid the broken glass.

Mummy was still asleep. Her mouth had turned blue at the edges. 'Perhaps she is cold, 'Lucy thought. She touched her small hand to her mother's cheek. It was icy cold. Lucy retracted her hand, puzzled. Mummy had not moved or stirred at her touch. Perhaps Lucy could bring the sunshine in here; that would warm her up, might make her feel better.

She looked around the room, wondering what she could use to bring the sunshine in. An empty perfume bottle lay on its side on the dresser, thrown carelessly down with the combs, lipsticks and creams. Lucy couldn't remember ever seeing mummy use any of those things.

She scooped up the bottle and flew down the stairs, small and light on her feet. Innocently heedless of whoever might be watching, she skipped down the path and across the lawn in her flimsy nightdress. The top of the bottle was stiff, presenting a problem to her little fingers but it came open when she tried with her teeth.

Lucy smiled and held the bottle up, as high above her head as she could possibly reach; stretching up to the sun. The glass sparkled and glowed; she held it there until her arms ached. Then quickly, so as not to let out any of the sun she had captured, she screwed the lid back on and raced inside.

It took a while for her eyes to readjust to the dark interior of the house, causing her to slow down as she climbed the stairs this time. The bedroom was exactly as she had left it. Full of hope, Lucy climbed up on to the bed and showed her mother's closed eyes the bottle of sunshine.

Nothing happened. Perhaps she should open it and let the sunshine fill the room.

Lucy unscrewed the lid and held the bottle aloft, to allow the sun to spread as far as possible. Nothing happened again; no bright light, no warmth, no sunshine. Mummy's eyes didn't even flicker.

Disappointed, Lucy sat back on her heels, feeling her chilly feet against the warmth of her bare thighs under her nightdress. Now what?

A car was approaching. Lucy ran to the window and climbed up onto the dresser as she had many times before, to look out of the window. The van! The man with the shopping van was coming down the street!

Recklessly, Lucy raced downstairs a third time. The man would help her; he would come and wake mummy up!

She was out on the lawn, suddenly very afraid that he would not stop, after all; that he would go past, miss her somehow. She had to go closer, onto the pavement; onto the road. Anything to make him see her and stop.

She ignored the grit stinging her bare feet, ignored the grazing on her knees when she stumbled and fell. She had to get him to stop; *she had to.*

It was more important to Lucy than even she understood.

Cain wasn't concentrating on the road; he didn't see the strange little kid until it was too late. He had been texting a friend. He knew it was ok; the roads around here were usually dead, especially at this time of day. It wasn't like he would do it anywhere busy.

Yet when he looked up, there she was; kneeling in the middle of the road like the scrawny ghost of a scruffy little beggar.

She was looking straight up at him, with a sad kind of smile on her face. That was the one thing that stayed with him forever after; the thing that haunted his dreams.

When he explained to the police for what felt like the thousandth time; when the paper and T.V people pressed him for a comment, blood-thirsty vultures that they were, it was that image that flooded his mind. Not the memory of the sickening thud as the van slammed into her tiny frame. Not the deep lurch in his stomach when he felt the impact. Not even his utter repulsion and physical sickness when he got out of the van, shocked and shaken, and saw what was left of Lucy.

For that was her name; he hadn't even been aware that he knew it. He must have heard it sometime before, when he had made deliveries here before. He'd dredged it up out of his memory in that fractional, numb space before the horror of what he had done finally hit home.

It was none of that that came to him, when asked what he could recall.

Just that smile. That sad smile; too old and far too heavy for such a skinny little kid.

The tree shook as a delicious vibration travelled its length. Its' luxurious leaves rustled in murmured approval. To the observant onlooker, it would have appeared for a moment to have stretched; strong arms reaching triumphantly to a clear blue sky. Or to have swelled somehow; its girth thickening, just as an arrogant man might puff out his chest vainly. That same observer would most likely have dismissed it as a trick of the light, or of the eye, or both.

Yet stretch and swell the old oak did; as if immensely proud of something.

Once again, the night throws its blanker over Oakwood Close. Its occupants begin to wrap up in their own, personal cocoons, imagining themselves unassailable. The oak tree stands in dominion over the houses, content to allow these transient mortals their veneer of security. It is too old, too wise and too elemental to show them otherwise. It is anyway beyond its abilities. There is only one way in which the tree can touch their fleeting lives; the only way it needs.

Succour: to draw from their fears and desires, lusts and revulsions as it draws moisture from the earth.

It has stood many ages of man; ignored, revered, tolerated, patronised. Yet here it still stands. Mighty now, with the strength of sapped souls; vitalised by energies that were never meant to be released. Grasping the earth with greedy, searching fingers that can never be prised free.

In the depths of the night an acorn tumbles, almost playfully, from a bough. It taps, branch to branch, as if calling on neighbours to bid them goodbye as it falls. The boughs wave in return, bidding their young farewell.

The night is soft and perfect. The acorn strokes the lowest branch and falls to the ground, rolling and bouncing.

A squirrel streaks across the grass, disobeying the most primitive instincts which are screaming at it to turn away. It scoops up the acorn and scampers off. Away, away; streets and woods away. Fields away, before the acorn releases it and it turns on its bushy tail and melts, terrified, into the shelter of the dark woods.

The fruit of the oak rocks gently in the cradle of soil into which it was dropped. There is nothing here yet, just a field in an open space on the edge of a town. In time, man will come here. He will build his makeshift houses and imagine he is master. No matter; the oak will be here.

Waiting.

THE SANDMAN

Martin could not put it off any longer; for the sake of some kind of normality, he had to go up to bed.

The thought made him feel sick. The sheer terror that the prospect instilled in him made him want to weep.

He rubbed his eyes, ran a hand over his bristly chin. Exhausted as he was, he knew he did not have a restful night's sleep ahead. Sighing in resignation, he heaved himself up, flicked off the living room light and stepped into the hallway.

The house was quiet, as might be expected at this time of night. There was the low hum of the heating, left running. The knocks and bangs every house makes as it settles, but nothing untoward at all. To an outside observer, Martin's reluctance would not be easy to explain.

It wasn't that he could not bear to be close to Lucy; he

wanted nothing more. The simple, unaffected pleasure of being able to lie with his arms around his wife, for them to fall asleep together, was something he was almost willing to kill for now.

He didn't dare to touch her, shrinking from any contact beneath the warmth of the sheets; terrified of tainting her with his affliction. She didn't understand; how could she? He had seen the look of hurt on her face when he had fed her excuse after excuse for the things he was doing, the crazed look in his eyes. Increasingly wild and unlikely, he had finally cashed in all the little excuses for the real biggie and cited depression. It was horrible, it was deceitful and it was low, but it had worked.

The D word not only offered some explanation for his odd behaviour, but had removed all of Lucy's weapons too. How could she berate him now? Such a diagnosis meant she had to be supportive, she had to understand; most of all, she had to back off.

He felt terrible doing it to her, but he really had no choice.

Martin felt the beginnings of a headache throb at his temple. He shuffled to the foot of the stairs like a man condemned and rested a shaking hand on the rail. So far, so good.

He set his foot on the bottom stair and closed his eyes in defence against the inevitable. He felt it almost immediately; the merest shimmer of tiny, hard grains rubbing against the sole of his foot.

He stepped up to the next stair, the sensation against his skin growing in intensity. By the fifth step, there was no doubt about it, had Martin had any doubt remaining; a fine layer of sand lined both of his slippers.

Martin let out a small moan, biting his finger between his teeth in a bid to stop it becoming a wail. When would this nightmare ever end?

He ploughed on. By the time he reached the top step, sand encased his feet within his slippers and rubbed against their tongues, making the skin beneath sore.

He stopped at the top. The landing stretched between him and the bathroom. Only a few feet away, it might as well have been a galaxy the way Martin felt. He had tried to run it before and found that made things far worse. The sand simply became so heavy and deep that it slowed his gait to a near-standstill and left him panicked and marooned on the landing. So now he willed himself not to run; easy does it, until he reached the sanctuary of the bathroom.

The bathroom; his one glimmer of hope. If he could just get there unhindered, he could begin to put his plan into action.

It was a feeble plan at best, he knew; but it was all he could come up with. Night after night of enduring the supernatural sand that marked his passage to bed, Martin had noticed one small thing that might work in his favour; it stopped pouring into his slippers and surrounding his feet when he reached the bathroom door.

That knowledge offered such relief to Martin that he considered telling Lucy he would sleep in the bath from now on. He very nearly suggested it to her, reasoning that at least she wouldn't have to put up with his restlessness, tossing and turning at night.

Something had cautioned him to keep his mouth shut. His marriage was close to ruin already, without him spending his nights in the bath.

If he told Lucy the real truth she would think he was insane and probably leave him anyway.

It didn't bear thinking about.

He had made it to the bathroom. He almost fell over its threshold, shutting and locking the door behind him. He looked around him; the red bin that always stood next to the toilet was in its usual place.

He took off his slippers and emptied them of sand, shaking them into the bin. He rubbed his feet clean with a hand towel, throwing it into the wash basket before tying the handles of the bag inside the bin, pulling it out and dropping it into the sink.

This plan had to work; he was all out of ideas otherwise.

He picked up the bin and held it under the cold water tap on the bath. Holding his breath, he suddenly realised he didn't even know if it would hold water.

He watched closely as it began to fill. No drips escaped; it seemed to hold firm. He was careful not to fill it to the rim. He didn't want water spilling over the edge and giving him away. Everything had to appear normal when He came. At least, what passed for normal in this house.

Martin put his slippers back on. Out on to the landing; the part he hated most.

Holding the bin as steadily as he could, Martin steeled himself to go on. He knew exactly how many steps it would take him to reach his bedroom; five. Five long, unending steps.

He had to do it. Just as he knew they would, his slippers began to slowly refill with sand, pouring through his toes like so many dry worms. He tried not to squirm but couldn't stop himself; the sand tickled unpleasantly.

By the time he reached his bedroom, sand was spilling out from his slippers. Martin knew the worst was yet to come.

He crossed to the bed and looked down at his sleeping wife; she appeared rested and untroubled. Why?

He kicked his slippers off, as far under the bed as he could, enjoying the feel of carpet on his bare toes; softer and more forgiving than sand. He undressed quickly, knowing it would not feel like carpet for long.

He left his boxer shorts on and eased into bed, making sure his hand gripped the edge of the water-filled bin. He lay back onto cool cotton sheets that smelled of something fresh and delicately floral and inhaled deeply.

The light, pleasant scent of flowers dissipated; now he smelled salt on the air, the coolness of freshening sea winds.

Sand.

He had known it would come. Gone were the crisp, clean bed sheets. He was lying on sand, feeling it grind and shift beneath his weight. He was afraid to close his eyes; didn't dare to close them. They flitted restlessly across the room, taking in the curtains swaying gently in the heat rising from the radiator.

As he watched them they blurred and distorted,

changing from the sunflower yellow Lucy had picked out so carefully, to shades of green. They flapped in the gathering breeze, their texture now changing, becoming smooth and shiny, until he was no longer looking at innocuous bedroom curtains but at the leaves of a palm tree, rustling in the wind.

He must have closed his eyes; he was slipping away from the room, from his wife. There was no hope for it now.

With something akin to relief he sagged against his sandy bed and waited for Him to come.

He didn't have to wait long.

When this had first begun, just a few short weeks ago, Martin had thought it was merely a vivid dream. He had always imagined the Sandman (when he thought of him, which was almost never; then) as a sort of Father Christmas in a yellow suit, carrying a sack full of sand rather than toys. He imagined he would sprinkle the stuff liberally into the stubborn eyes of wakeful children; forcing them to close and thus, to sleep. The reality, if that's what it was, was very different.

An image had presented itself to him that first night as he lay on his gritty bed. All around him was sand; from far away came the subdued to and fro roar of a sea, though he was yet to lay eyes on it. All he had been able to see were those swaying palm leaves and endless sand, stretching for miles; forever, for all he knew. A curious voice had addressed him, sometimes soft and cool, then harsh and rasping.

"Martin,"

He had looked, past his feet as he reclined; at nothing at first, until at last He had shown Himself.

He appeared to pour upwards until dry sand stood tall in the loose shape of a man. Arms and legs were all there. The face bore two mismatched shells for eyes, dried out kelp arranged as a lop-sided mouth. No nose, Martin noticed absurdly.

"Martin," The Sandman repeated softly, "Why aren't you sleeping Martin? Why? Tell me; why aren't you sleeping?

Martin was unable to speak. His mouth was dry, his tongue wooden. He wanted to shout, "Put your sand in my eyes and not in my slippers then!" But he couldn't utter a word. The Sandman's purpose seemed malicious; to keep him awake, not send him to sleep.

That was exactly what he had done, every night since. Martin had lost so much sleep that in the end he had to give up work. It was just too dangerous; he had almost fallen asleep at the wheel of his lorry more than once. He had promised Lucy that it would just be temporary, until he sorted himself out. Back then he was still unsure if he was suffering nothing more than a recurring bad dream, if it was real, or if he was going mad. He still wasn't sure.

Tonight was going to be no different it seemed; except that now he knew what to expect.

As if on cue there came that odd rasping voice in his ear.

"Martin?" That hoarse, insistent voice and then there He was, standing at his feet, shell eyes and seaweed mouth leering, sand arms gesticulating impossibly in the air, "Still awake Martin? What will we do with you?" A sound like gravel sliding down paper; Martin guessed it to be laughter.

Gathering his courage, Martin forced his gaze left to the bin full of water. It was still there, his fingers touching its rim, its bright red plastic incongruous in these surroundings. So far, so good.

The Sandman did not appear to have noticed. He was persisting in his dry litany of mocking questions. Could he really see out of those shell eyes? Martin wondered. He pushed himself up onto his elbows, expecting some sort of punishment for this act of defiance; a face full of stinging sand maybe, or gritty hands pushing him down.

Nothing; the Sandman simply continued in his questioning. A wave of hysteria threatened to engulf Martin and he had to suppress a laugh; was he trying to bore him to sleep?

"Why aren't you sleeping Martin? Can't you find your way to the Land of Nod?" That brittle laugh again, "Bright-eyed and bushy tailed, that's you!"

As he had listened, his gaze focused on the Sandman, Martin had shifted position, achingly slowly. Now he was on his knees, the bucket in his hands. He realised that his bed had gone; as had his bedroom. He was no longer in those comfortable, homely surroundings. He wasn't kneeling on his soft old mattress; his wife was not lying beside him.

There was nothing but sand around him, as far as the eye could see; the backdrop the blackest of skies, as endless as the sand.

Should he try it now?

The Sandman paused mid-sentence; something he had never done before. Martin froze, the salt-wind stinging his lips, his thumping heartbeat echoing in his head. The moment seemed to stretch on for an eternity. With a silty sigh, the Sandman resumed his taunting.

Martin waited for his heartbeat to return to near normal, before cautiously rising to his feet. The Sandman was tall; Martin saw he was at least a foot shorter.

Was there enough water? The bin suddenly seemed small and silly. Martin had to fight off the urge to give up, lie down and submit himself to the Sandman once more. The feeling passed. Trying to steady his shaking hands, Martin lifted the bin into the air,

Water lapped against its sides, making a wet, slapping noise. The Sandman stopped again, hands frozen in mid-air, shells eyes definitely *looking at Martin.*

"A bucket" The Sandman crooned as if delighted, "Going to build a castle?" The question was innocent, its tone full of menace, "Going to make a *big* castle, with battlements and flags and all?" The Sandman was quivering, his legs threatening to crumble beneath him. He appeared angry.

Martin clutched the bin to his chest, trying to hold it steady, his hands weak with fear.

"Going to protect it, are you? Make good, strong walls? Maybe dig out a *moat?*" The word was a roar, like rocks clashing, "Water eh? Well it took you long enough Martin. Think I am easy to beat, do you? Well, you have to find me first!"

Then he was gone.

Martin felt sick. He was alone with the ridiculous red bin, the sand, the inky blackness and that palm tree, wafting its leaves gently in the breeze. How was he supposed to find the Sandman here? More to the point; where could he be hiding? There was nowhere to go, no sign of movement…

Except for that tree.

The only feature in this flat, weird landscape. It had to be significant. Martin wracked his brains, trying to work out how.

What do you think of when you think of palm trees? Coconuts? Holiday? That made no sense.

And then he understood; life.

That tree was the only thing in this miserable desert that was alive and growing. The realisation offered comfort; Martin resolved not to move too far from it.

He set the bin down carefully at the tree's base and chose a direction to start from; west, as far as he could tell. He stuck out a foot, suddenly feeling very exposed in only his boxer shorts. He had the sense that thousands of eyes were upon him. Irrationally, he wished he had pockets to shove his hands into.

The sand was gritty but firm beneath his feet. Growing in confidence he ventured out further and immediately regretted it. Clammy hands shot up and grabbed him. Made only of sand and stone, those hands were as strong as any man's. Martin screamed and sat down heavily, straining to resist being pulled under. He dug his fists in behind him and heaved backwards with all his strength, terrified He might grab his hands too…

The thought gave him extra strength. He heaved back with all his might until the grip weakened, then was released altogether.

Martin hurriedly tucked his feet beneath him, panting with shock and exertion. Not going that way then.

He rose and staggered to the tree. The leaves had begun to wave more fervently in the wind. Was it his imagination, or did they seem now to be growing lower down its trunk?

Tentatively, Martin stretched up. He could reach one. The branch it grew upon felt light and dry. It snapped off easily.

It had seemed the right thing to do, but now that Martin held the branch in his hand he had no idea what to do with it. He sat down, leaning against the trunk, careful not to upset the bucket, and pondered over it. Nothing came to him. Exasperated, he threw it out across the sand stretching to his left; eastward.

A sandy white hand shot out and pulled the branch below.

A green leaf gently slapped against Martin's face.

Another branch, so low down that he could reach it from a sitting position? Martin was certain it had not been there before.

An idea formed in Martin's mind.

He faced forwards, north as far he could determine,

and threw the second branch. Again, the sandy white hand flashed out. Building his hopes up, he turned southward, snapped off another obliging branch and threw it as far as he could.

Again, the sand-hand snatched it under.

He was trapped here then, in this not so idyllic oasis. For it *was* an oasis; a palm tree, its shade and a bin full of water.

Martin began to laugh; found he could not stop. He laughed a loud, breath-taking, belly aching laugh, until his ribs hurt; until he cried.

"What's so funny Martin?"

Martin stopped dead, though his fear had inexplicably lessened. He was listening carefully, trying to pinpoint the Sandman's location, for he had not shown himself yet; was merely whispering from the shale and grains.

He was close, Martin knew that much.

"Still not a sleepy boy?" The Sandman's voice came from behind him.

Martin found his own, "Why don't you come closer Mr Sandman? Where I can see you? Where we can talk properly?"

That grating, rasping laugh. But Martin was wondering now; *why doesn't he come any closer?*

What was it here that the Sandman feared?

He turned to the tree again. Not just the red bin full of tap water surely?

Why hadn't those dry, flaky hands shot up from the sand in the immediate area of this tree? Was it really an oasis, after all? *Was that what the Sandman was afraid of?*

The tree, strange though it was, was thriving. Even this tree must need water, Martin reasoned. So where was it getting it from?

He began to form a theory. Estimating roughly the centre of his odd oasis, he dropped to his knees and began to dig with his bare hands, looking for water like he used to when he was a kid at the beach. If it was there at all, it was buried deep. Martin felt a cool sheen of sweat on his back and his brow and was about to give up hope, when his fingertips dipped into the unmistakable coolness of water.

He had been right. It hadn't been such a crazy idea to bring the bin full of water along with him; the Sandman was afraid of water!

That was why he had stopped short of invading his bathroom when he invaded Martin's home at night. Suddenly, it made a sort of crazy sense.

Gritting his teeth, Martin worked to expand the hole he had made. He was gratified to see that it filled quickly, becoming quite deep. Gripping the trunk of the palm with one hand, he gingerly dipped his foot into the small well he had created, trying to estimate how deep it was.

The water came to his knee, but his foot hadn't reached the soft bed he had expected it to yet. He pressed on, the water coming up to his thigh, wetting the edge of his boxer shorts. This couldn't be right; he hadn't dug that deeply.

He yanked his leg out, back onto dry land, suspicious that perhaps there *was* no floor to that particular pool; nothing else was normal here.

He sat against the tree once more and got his breath

back. He would go back to his original plan then; he had a seemingly endless supply of water here at his disposal. He trod warily, estimating just how far the perimeter of the tree afforded him some sort of protection. He could make out a faint impression in the sand, marking out where he had been resting when he had first 'arrived.' He crossed to the spot now and knelt like a runner about to start a race; one knee raised, the other knee flat, hands braced in front, poised. He hoped that his straying away from the source of water would be enough to tempt the Sandman to come back and resume his taunting.

He reappeared almost immediately, confirming Martin's sense that he had been watching the whole time. He launched into his tedious tirade straight away, as if he couldn't wait to berate him.

"That's right Martin; give in. You know there is nowhere you can go now, don't you? Why don't you just give in, and close your eyes?"

To Martin's bemusement, the Sandman began to approximate singing, sawing out the words of lullaby, *"Go to sleep, go to sleep, go to sleep little Martin…"*

Martin shut out the noise and concentrated on edging slowly closer to the bin, which he had placed a foot or two behind him, keeping his runner pose the whole time. The Sandman appeared not to notice and was repeating the monotonous refrain over and over. Now and then he danced a grotesque, jerking little jig, as if celebrating victory. Then he would fall still again and take up the tune.

Martin had reached the bin. He picked it up in one smooth motion and lurched forward, desperate not to be reckless in his aim. As accurately as he was able, he flung the contents of the bin forwards and upwards, at the Sandman's face.

It was a hit, but only just; enough to take the Sandman by surprise. Martin raced to the well, dipped the bucket in it, then returned to his vantage point and threw again.

This time he hit his target full on. The top of the Sandman's head sloshed away, his remaining eye left to slide down his grainy face. Martin did not pause to watch. He refilled the bucket and threw again, sending the shoulder and left arm flying, to disintegrate into thin air. Another bucketful; another, and another. The well never seemed to grow any shallower. The Sandman's body parts dissolved into the dark background until he was completely gone, nothing more than wet clumps of sand dotted about to bear witness to Martin's frenzied attack.

Martin himself was covered in sand; in his hair, up his wrists and ankles and worst of all, in his mouth. The thought that it might be part of the Sandman was sickening. He lurched to the well and half jumped, half fell into it, forgetting his earlier caution, just desperate to feel his skin clean and smooth once more.

He was surprised to find the water was not at all salty. It had lost its earlier coldness and was now invitingly warm. He opened his arms and legs wide, allowing it full access to his dry, aching body. He luxuriated in it. He took a breath and submerged himself in it, rejoicing in its wonderful refreshment.

And he felt himself being pulled swiftly and inexorably downwards. He panicked, afraid of drowning after all he had just survived; until he realised that he was screaming. He could hear his own voice, under water. If he was screaming, then he must be breathing…

There was a rush of warm air, and then Martin landed. He felt a wooden surface beneath him but the landing had not hurt him; it was not hard or uncomfortable. He allowed his body to relax a little, a gentle rocking motion lulling him into calmness.

He sat up and looked about him. He was in a small boat; a blue-black sky littered with stars loomed above him. All around him were boats like his, gently rocking to and fro.

Something white was zigzagging down towards him. Instinctively he lay back, watching its descent. IT swung a few graceful curves before landing softly upon him; a warm, cotton sheet smelling of something delicate and floral. Then there was a pillow beneath his head, the rocking motion of the boat became more insistent, the stars twinkled reassuringly above. Unable to fight it, Martin closed his eyes, and went to sleep.

He awoke in the early afternoon in his own bed. There were no tell-tale grains of sand, not even in his slippers. His boxer shorts were dry. The curtains were sunflower yellow. The red bin was in the bathroom, next to the toilet

Everything was all right.

He had won.

Not bothering to dress, Martin threw on his dressing

gown and went down stairs. He had expected to find the kids were at school, his wife at work, some sort of sarcastic note as to his laziness on the kitchen table. Instead, he found his family all huddled together on the sofa, still in nightclothes, the old quilt used in illness and emergency draped over them.

"What's up with you lot?" He felt unaccountably chirpy.

"Good to see you finally had a good night's sleep," his wife evaded his question, but he didn't like the edge to her voice.

There was something wrong here; he could sense it.

"Never mind me; what's wrong?"

"Oh, nothing really, it's just ironic isn't it, that none of *us* could sleep a wink last night?"

"But you were all sound asleep when I came up,"

"Really? Well like I said, funny,"

"Why?"

"Well we all woke up at pretty much the same time. Sammy and the girls came in to me practically together, no much past midnight. And none of us could get back off. I sent the girls back to bed and cuddled up with Sam but we were all wide awake. And *you* weren't in bed, Martin," her tone accusing, "So where were you?"

Martin was stunned. He could think of nothing to say. It had never occurred to him that he might need a ready excuse. He had woken in his own bed after all. Where else could he have been?

It had never crossed his mind that he physically left that bedroom.

"All these weeks skiving off work, complaining about tiredness. No wonder you're always tired! Something's keeping you up all night and it sure as hell isn't me Martin!"

Kelly, their oldest daughter, threw back the quilt and gave her father a look that was a mixture of disgust and disbelief. She marched out of the room and up the stairs.

Martin turned back to Lucy, struggling to find the words that would make sense here.

From the hallway, Kelly shrieked, "Dad! *Dad!* Quick, come here!

Martin raced out into the hall, grateful for a moment's distraction. Kelly was sitting on the stairs a few steps up, holding her pink slippers in her hands. She looked confused.

"What is it love?" Martin asked, his churning stomach telling him he already knew.

"Look!" she said in a small voice, upturning her slippers to let out a stream of white-gold sand.

Martin pinched himself hard, to be sure he wasn't still dreaming.

But it hurt.

DEVIL'S DROP

The twin caves protruded from the innocent Welsh earth like fathomless eye sockets from a dark skull. Liquid, black and viscous, shimmered in the depths of one as if weeping to rid itself of some irritant. Indeed the crest of a slow wave bore a sheep, dead, bloated and obscene, down upon the sharp cave walls, slicing it open and releasing the pent-up gases of mortem in the swollen body like the bursting of a tainted rain-cloud.

If this was a huge skull, the remains perhaps of some ancient giant, then the nose had long ago corroded, leaving only a deep murky pool in its place. On the surface mirror smooth and dark, beneath stirred a grim soup of torn tree limbs, pitiful strips of ragged, rough-sewn cloth, animal carcasses and ghostly, bloodless flesh.

The trees grew away from the caves, reaching for all their worth for the reassurance of the sunlight above and the illusion of safety in their numbers. The rich ground beneath them teemed with fungi, mosses and countless scrabbling creatures, petering out to become nothing more than a barren border of mud around the caves. Even the birds kept their distance, darting in nervously to snatch a grub or a berry only when they dared. And always the dark waters of the skull licked luridly at the walls of their prison, causing dull, muted thumps to echo round the caves as nameless things collided in their depths.

Beyond the wood a few scattered houses dotted the gentle hills, specks of lamp light here and there serving only to accentuate the darkness. In those humble dwellings people slept, only occasionally enduring restless, fitful nights of snatched sleep punctured by the inexplicable need to pray for deliverance from some elemental dread. The people never spoke of this, just as they never spoke of the need to empty their bowels or to die.

Deep in the earth, below the sightless cave eyes and the fetid, nostril waters, the skull grinned.

Mam had allowed her to finish her chores a little earlier today, so that she might take her little brother to collect holly for the Midwinter celebrations. Even so, the sun was already low in the sky and beginning to redden.

With the sensitive little Morvran in earshot, their mother spoke only to issue a reminder to be home soon. Rhiannon knew, by the look her mother gave her and from countless warnings received throughout her childhood so far, that they were to stay well away from Devil's Drop.

Like most of the village children, Rhiannon had from time to time ignored the warnings, which served only to make the woods an even more intriguing place to explore, and had secretly gone there with a brave friend or two. She knew because of these adventures, though she would never tell her mother, that it was the closest place to find good holly. Acknowledging her mother's unspoken admonishment with a nod, Rhiannon had nonetheless decided she would go there with Morvran now; they wouldn't go too near Devil's Drop itself and they wouldn't stay long. It was true that the place had a feel about it that made her uncomfortable but, she decided, she and Morvran would be safe enough. Good Spirits lived amongst the holly leaves after all; wasn't that why she was gathering them in the first place?

The wicker basket they had brought was filling fast with glistening green boughs, spotted with red berries like spatterings of blood. Rhiannon paused in her search for the best branches, shivered and drew her shawl more closely around her. Morvran had given up picking the holly, having scratched his hands repeatedly, and was beginning to whine.

"Come on Rhiannon, let's go home now. Mam will wonder where we are,"

"All right Morvran, I won't be long."

"Now Rhiannon, please? I'm bored and my hands are sore,"

Morvran pouted, held out his hands as if to prove his injuries were real and then crossed his arms petulantly, causing Rhiannon to giggle at his defiance. He was such a sweet little boy, she thought. "All right, just one or two more and I'll stop, I promise. Why don't you go and sit by the tree there and wait for me? I'll give you a ride home on my back if you like; if you promise not to sulk."

"All the way?" he asked, his pout vanishing.

"All the way,"

Morvran considered this, then nodded his agreement and scuffed his way over to the old tree to sit cross-legged on a ruptured root.

"Good boy," Rhiannon smiled.

Something behind her caused her to turn, her small knife thrust before her in a feeble gesture of defence. An abrupt unease permeated the rapidly cooling early evening, but there was nothing to be seen. The sudden sense of a presence, seen or not, unnerved her though; Morvran was right, they should leave now. She was about to call to him that they were going after all when, as if to deliberately persuade her to stay, an exceptionally beautiful bough of holly danced in the breeze, drawing her attention and distracting her from her concerns. The firm leaves were a dark, rich shade of green and the berries were as warm as the reddest wine. What spirits must abide in those branches! To leave them growing there was unthinkable now that she had spotted them; it would only take a little longer to cut them down. Besides, Mam would be thrilled, she knew.

Resolved, Rhiannon put down her basket and carefully edged her way up to the bush. It was growing to the left of and slightly above Devil's Drop. The muddy edge fringing the skull would be dry and dusty in the summer months, but now it was slick and wet with sodden earth and Rhiannon had trouble keeping her footing. Trying not to alarm the watching Morvran, Rhiannon knew immediately she took her next step that she had misjudged it. She lost her hold and slipped; dropping the sharp little blade she had been using and grasping wildly at the holly bush for a handhold, shredding her hands in the process. The knife bounced and tumbled, slipping into the oily water below with barely a splash.

Morvran sat up in alarm as Rhiannon cried out, hauling herself up on the piercing foliage somehow, regaining her balance and her foothold. Her hands were bleeding; she was shaking violently, her legs weak with shock. It took great effort to call down to Morvran, trying to hide her fear, "Scared you, did I?"

A globule of blood, freshly harvested from Rhiannon's shredded palms and bare wrists, gathered in a cradling leaf of the holly bush, quickly became too heavy a burden and dripped below, silent and unnoticed.

"Rhiannon, let's go now, please. I don't like it here. It's getting dark." Morvran pleaded, adding as an afterthought, as if it might make his sister consider him more seriously, "Besides, I'm hungry. I want to go home."

"Trust you to think of your stomach! I don't know where you put it all Morvran, there's nothing to you boy!" She was trying to make light of things, to fool herself as well as Morvran that all was well. But he was right; it had become too dark too quickly and the atmosphere had changed, not just with the drop in temperature as the day grew late, but in another, more repressive way. The very air felt heavy on her shoulders. The holly bough that only moments ago had so beguiled her now seemed no more appealing than any she had already gathered.

"All right, enough is enough. I'm coming back down."

The little boy sighed in relief and stood, hugging himself through his tunic in an effort to keep warm in the growing coldness. He squinted through the encroaching gloom, anxiously watching his sister's descent and willing her to move more quickly.

Rhiannon gingerly disentangled herself from the holly bush, her hands scratched and sore. She turned to face the treacherous slope that led back to her brother. She felt exposed here; as if she had allowed herself to become vulnerable to something she could not identify.

"What?" She said, pausing.

"What do you mean, *what?*" Morvran asked, bemused. Rhiannon heard a new note of fear creep into his voice.

"You said something."

"I never said anything!" Morvran protested, "Come on Rhiannon, I want to go!"

Rhiannon's face turned a deathly pallor, "But I heard you!" she whispered, "I heard a voice. Didn't you hear it Morvran?"

"No!" Morvran shouted, "You're scaring me Rhiannon! I'll tell Mam! You shouldn't frighten me like that. We shouldn't have come here anyway! I'll tell on you I will!" Unable to contain it any longer, the tired and terrified little boy broke down in tears.

A voice more felt than heard, blossomed into the night like a dark bloom, blackly seductive.

"Bringer of blood, bringer of tears; be as one with me," A mist of breath, white and writhing, rose up from the pool and hung on the air, shifting, climbing, dissolving.

"I want Mam!" Morvran gasped, as if for him now the very act of breathing was a struggle. "I want Mam now! I want to go home now!" Distraught and terrified, Morvran did not notice the urgent stream of urine that had escaped his bladder and was now darkening the front of his tunic and leggings and pooling beneath his feet.

"Bringer of blood, bringer of tears, bringer of essence; be as one with me," The mist of breath rose again.

Rhiannon, frozen on her slippery platform, could only utter a weak "No!"

Helpless at the base of the skull, Morvran seemed to her so very small and alone. Why had she come here? Why? She knew this was no place to be; to bring Morvran. This was all her fault.

"It's all right Morvran, cariad. It's all right! Go back to the basket, where we put the holly we picked. The good spirits will still be in there, in the holly leaves! They'll keep you from harm," Even as she said it she knew it to be untrue; whatever spirits dwelt in the holly were no match for this nameless evil. She was surrounded by holly bushes up here wasn't she? Yet she knew instinctively that she wasn't safe. She prayed the little boy would not think of that. "You'll be safe enough then; just get to the basket."

"I can't!"

"Yes you can! You *can* Morvran; I'm coming too, see?" She took a wary step, "I'll meet you there, at the basket. You just have to try; you just have to move your legs! It' gone now, listen? Nothing! Look; the mist has gone, you see? It was just mist and now it's gone!" Another lie; please Morvran, please don't argue with me; not now, not here "On you go, there's a good boy. I'm following look." Rhiannon forced her feet back into sluggish action, trying not to misplace them again on the precarious ledge, praying to all the spirits of the woods and the Earth that the voice would not speak again, that she would not slip a second time.

A laugh, as hollow and as deep as the caves themselves, reverberated around them.

Morvran's crying, already wretched, fell away completely in his horror, only to become a wail when he caught his next stuttered breath; a desperate, formless entreaty. Rhiannon nearly joined him in his despair, the need to concentrate and to watch her footing all that kept her from it. What would Mam say when she got him home? What would Dad do? How could she have been so stupid? Would she get home? Would she see Mam and Dad again? Suddenly, it was not as inevitable as it had earlier been. What in the name of Mother Earth was happening here?

"Stop it!" Rhiannon shouted, a wave of violent and unexpected anger overtaking her, "Stop it now, whatever you are! Leave him alone! He's just a baby, that's all! Leave him alone! Leave *us* alone!" Her voice reached a shrieking pitch which left her throat sore.

The laughter faded. Morvran's hysteria reduced to hurried, shallow breaths. They both fell anxiously silent, waiting for some reaction. Nothing happened, but Rhiannon's instincts screamed at her to hurry; at once convinced that they had little time left to waste. It was not over.

"Morvran, get to the basket! *Now* Morvran; run!"

Despite his fear, Morvran did as he was bid, the command in his sister's voice not to be ignored. The wicker basket looked heavy and awkward in his small hands. "Good boy," she said, weakly encouraging, "Now then, turn around; it's all right I'm watching you. I want you to start back, all right? Go back to the field, where we came in. You know where I mean? Where I pick mushrooms sometimes for Mam?"

"What about you?" his eyes were wide in his pale face, his nose running unchecked and his soiled garments sagging heavily as if ashamed to be near him.

He's just a baby. Leave him alone!

"I'm fine Morvran. I'm just being careful that's all. This path is slippery; no good me falling now, is it? I'll catch you up. Go on."

"But then what do I do?"

"What do you mean?"

"When I get to the field; do I wait for you then? What should I do?"

A sensation shimmered over Rhiannon; the lightest brush of something across her cheek, down the soft skin at her throat. The suggestion of a warm breath on her neck made her flesh rise and the delicate hairs on her young neck stand on end. If she had been a woman she might have likened it to the sensuous touch of a lover, but she was a girl still, and this caress left her feeling tainted, dirty and sick to her stomach. A stirring in the pool below caught her eye; something sluggish in the grey and black of the water turned its pallid expression upwards, to look directly at her. Rhiannon stifled a scream, unable to comprehend what she was seeing, her mind threatening instead to become numb to thought. What is that? What in the name of all that is light and good is that? Afraid as she was to continue looking, she didn't dare tear her eyes away.

"No, Morvran, don't wait for me. You'll be able to see the village lights from the field, it's not far then. Just keep your eye on the lights and keep going, all right? Just run Morvran; run all the way home!"

THE CENTURY MAN

He placed the lid back on the shoebox as reverently as if he were replacing the lid of a coffin, sliding it carefully back under the bed. He knew it wasn't the proper way to store them but for now there was nothing he could do; he would find a way to keep his treasures safe, keep them whole. Absently rubbing his chin, he realised he needed a shave again. Wearily he padded into the bathroom. The light over the mirror was cruel, illuminating clearly the dark shadows under his eyes; his sallow, drawn skin, the near-grey hair that used to be a closely cropped black. It allowed no illusions and he had to admit that he was showing signs of ageing. He stared intently at his image, deep in thought; as if he expected his reflection to offer some explanation. It merely mocked him, aping his every move. How could he look so old, so tired, at his age? He grimaced. He knew only too well how, but who would ever believe him? He reached for the razor on the shelf above the sink. He had developed a taste for this cut-throat blade; had become comfortable with it. It was heavy and felt real and reliable in his hand; not light and ineffectual like the plastic disposable razors he used to favour. They kept their distance at work. It used to hurt him, make him angry. Now, he was grateful that they ignored him. It meant that he didn't have to find explanations, or answer awkward questions. They didn't even bother with insults anymore. He knew they still talked about him; he saw their wary looks. He also knew he perplexed them; he had changed so much since he started working there. He had become a different, much older, man. One of the gossips had started a rumour that he was suffering from some awful disease that aged him prematurely. This seemed to be widely accepted as true, though no-one ever asked him outright. Why? Were they afraid of him now? He believed that maybe they were. He hoped they were. This alone gave him great satisfaction. He remembered the day he started there, not such a long time ago. The minute he had set foot in the place he felt they had all known, instinctively, that there was something wrong about him. Nothing they could name or identify; it was beyond their comprehension. He had managed, unbelievably, to hide it for a while, but then the inevitable had happened; he had given himself away. There had been a magazine in the canteen, a '*man's*' magazine; the usual glossy mix of sex, satire and gritty realism. It had been left open at a two-page piece on a war raging in some small and obscure place, a place no one had heard of until the carnage had caught the world's attention. The text was informative and accurate, but it was the photographs that grabbed the eye; the scenes depicted in those shots were graphic, brutal and sickening. They had prompted comments from most of the people who saw them, about the waste and violence of war, the horror of it all. As well as, of course, the usual black humour that these things always seem to generate; the desperately unfunny jokes that everyone understands is just a way of putting some distance between themselves and the awful reality that's staring them in the face. They were all horrified by those pictures.All except him. He couldn't tear his eyes away from those images; he felt he could touch the fear, smell the blood in the air. He had been riveted, grinning a strange savage grin; devouring the scenes with his eyes. He felt a horrified fascination, a lust for more and at the same time he knew it was wrong; terribly, horribly wrong. He had managed to pull himself out of his trance, to find that the people who remained in the room were staring at him, disgusted. He realised he was actually drooling, saliva oozing from the side of his mouth. He wiped it hurriedly with the back of his sleeve, trembling as he did. He always felt like this when he knew he had been found out. His heart was pounding, his hands shaking. A feeling of guilty elation assailed him. He could wipe away the spittle, but the tight, dry grin stayed on his face. No one spoke. He turned to leave, excitement competing with fear and knotting his stomach. "You sick bastard," one of them muttered as he reached the door.He didn't turn around, didn't stop; he was still grinning as he left the room

He had held on to it for as long as he could; once he had given it that release, he found he couldn't hold it back any longer. It was as if a dam had broken and the force behind it was just too great.His 'workmates' stopped talking about events in the news, plots of films, the latest good book, while he was around. They all began to avoid him, recognising that there was something dark in him, something they didn't want to get too close to. The name calling and taunting, even threats, had lasted a while after the magazine thing; but he never bit back, never once allowed his temper to flare. He didn't believe he even had a temper, not like other people; just a sort of cold, inexplicable longing inside. They soon tired of it and settled for keeping a wide berth and deliberately excluding him. It didn't matter. He spent most of his time in daydreams; so lost that when he came back from them he could not have told you himself where he had been. He had no desire to hurt anyone; he merely wanted to be an observer, a witness, a shadow in the background. There was no room for that in these civilised days, no opportunity for blameless participation.

That was when the dreams began. At least, he had fooled himself that they were dreams. He knew now they were not; they could not have been. He had been lying fully dressed on his bed, drawing on a cigarette, idly blowing smoke rings in the air, wishing he had not been born here; not now. He felt he belonged to a different time, to a different place. Somewhere he would not stand out; where he would be just another man. He had no desire to be a great leader, a hero or even a villain; he just wanted to bear witness; to watch life's events, however big or small, passively. That would be more than enough for him. He stared resentfully at the ceiling, watching the smoke brush ineffectually against the dark wooden beams. A breeze rattled the loose sash window in its frame. The day was progressing; light was fading and rain spattered erratically on the roof above. He closed his eyes and tried to picture this house when it was new. He tried to imagine the sounds that would have reached him from the street then; imagining the smells the room might have held, listening for the hiss of gas lamps. Straining to see the flicker of a few well-placed candles; perhaps the crackle of a fire in the long-since blocked fireplace. He felt his eyes grow heavy and close; he was there. It was this very bedroom, but the wooden floorboards were now largely exposed, poorly covered by the sparsely strewn, threadbare rugs that dotted the floor. The window was closed tight and curtains drawn against it. A fire burned comfortingly in the grate; a single oil lamp glowed on a small bedside table. Two women busied about the room, one folding cloths, putting water to boil on the fire, warming towels. The other sat in a chair by the window, a small bundle in her arms. The weak and plaintive cry of a new-born child rose into the air; the woman hushed and soothed the infant, rocking her arms gently back and forth. A much younger woman lay in the bed, her colour high and her features worn, sweat-limp hair hanging close against her head and face. She was dressed all in white; nightdress knotted at the neck, tucked under crisp sheets of white cotton. But it was none of that that held him there. The busy woman was piling towels into a bucket, stirring the water to loosen stains from the towels. The clear water had turned blood red.

He woke up; or thought he woke. He wondered at his dream. It had seemed so real and yet this room had been so different. Then he realised that something had been the same. It had been raining there too; or *then*. He had been some kind of invisible spirit, watching the intimate, exhausted scene that the women had endured together; but they hadn't seen him. It was shortly after this that he had begun to fear he was going mad. The dreams were happening regularly and he had no control over them. Each time took him further back. He had witnessed that infant's beginnings long after the child had grown and died; and since then he had seen many other things. At first, all his visions were connected to the house. He witnessed one of its builders falling to his death before the house was completed. He had watched the attempted seduction of one of the housemaids; had seen that same attempt at seduction turn to rape, and that in turn to dismissal and to suicide. He had also seen the lady of the house turn a blind eye. Sometimes he was given pause, as if whoever, whatever, was showing him these things was giving him a chance to go back, to stop. When this happened he would lie and wait in anguish, afraid to move or breathe in case he caused to it all to end somehow. But the scenes always began to play out in front of his eyes eventually, like the play button had been pushed again. It was taking him further and further back. Now he saw the place before there was a house; when it was nothing more than a wide-open meadow. The river still ran through it, but the bridge was a crude wooden construction, not the neat brickwork that spanned it now. Then things changed; it started taking him to places that he did not know, to times so long ago no-one living could possibly remember them. He saw two men wearing tall white wigs, knee length trousers and stockinged feet, face one another in a duel. He watched one of the men turn and walk away, and the other collapse in a bloody heap; killed by the backfire from his own gun rather than by the bullet fired by his rival. He saw villages full of huts marked with crosses; disfigured, boil ridden people wailing in misery. He saw and smelt the funeral pyres burning. He watched thieves and robbers, muggers and arsonists about their work. Saw a field turn red with blood during a hacking battle that left both sides so defeated and slaughtered that it was impossible to tell who had won. It was wonderful! Liberating, breath-taking, glorious; all he had ever wanted. It was making him old. At first, he couldn't understand why. He convinced himself that he had only been a watcher, an observer. But things were not in his control. He would find himself waking, clutching something close to his chest, or tight in his hand. He would be ravaged with sweat and gasping for breath, his heart hammering behind his ribs. He had woken holding a musket, still warm from a shot; a bloody, short bladed knife; a heavy, wine stained goblet; a garrotte; a necklace of crudely carved amber and ivory, and many other things besides. How could he have got these things if he had been only an observer, protected by the distance of his real place in time? Slowly he began to accept that the dreams were more real than anyone would believe; he could not merely have been an observer. He was bringing these things back like trophies. He was *bringing them back*. It was beginning to show. The condensed time was still, nevertheless, time and the passage up and down the years was showing in his face. It was in the set of his shoulders; the gentle stoop in his back. He had begun to have his fill, but he knew of no way to stop it. Today he was very tired. His back and head were aching. He longed to sleep, but knew that he would not rest for it; he would awake more exhausted still. He had woken that morning to find he was holding a bone. He couldn't remember where he had got it from, or how, but he knew it was human. He had pulled his box full of treasures out from under the bed again, and carefully placed the bone inside it. He returned it to its hiding place, and climbed back into bed. He wouldn't go to work today; he didn't think anyone would care. They would probably be glad not to have him there. Besides, they wouldn't recognise him anymore. He tried so hard to resist it, but against his will, his eyes closed. He was *so* tired.

A circle of people; it was night-time, but the moon was whole and shining brightly above, bathing the world in a calm silver glow and casting strange shadows around him. The night was cold; he could hear the crackle and spit of a fire but couldn't see the flames or feel its heat. The air was heavy with subdued excitement. He looked around to see wild faces staring back at him. He realised he must be lying down; yes, now he could feel some unforgiving, uncomfortable surface beneath him. He shivered and attempted to cover himself better against the chill, only to find that his hands were bound in thick straps of hide and that he was anyway naked. For the first time in any of his dreams he felt a flicker of fear. He tried to hold back the rise in his throat, told himself that it was always all right; he always woke, safe in his bed. He had never been significant in his own dreams before. A low, sonorous chant had begun; it circled him and grew in strength as a figure drew closer. This man was also naked, with wild hair and mad eyes. He approached in circles; growing closer with every turn, shrieking and wailing in strange, guttural tones. He tried to plead for help, but his words came out as a stifled, unintelligible moan. The wild man had drawn close enough to touch now; looking down upon his helpless prey in a curious, birdlike way; then abruptly, he raised his hands to the sky. At once the chanting stopped; the only sound to break the silence was the still crackling fire. There was something oddly comforting about that sound, even now. The naked man screeched, a piercing, heart stopping noise. As if from nowhere a long thin blade appeared in his hand. He turned it, pointed it downwards, its wicked tip hovering above his victim's paralysed heart; slowly, he raised it higher, higher. The silence was tangible, filling the air. He could sense the eager anticipation of the circling onlookers; he recognised it, understood it, yet he feared it like never before. With another piercing, jubilant screech, the wild man drove the blade down with all his crazed strength. He saw his own blood fountain into his killer's face; saw it dripping off the altar into a slick pool on the wet earth. He smelled his own blood in the air; tasted the metallic tang of it in his mouth. He wished with all that was left of his heart that he could be one of the crowd looking on. Morning found him in bed, sheets tangled tightly around him. His death mask was one of sheer terror.

The landlady said she didn't know him, had never seen him before. She had a key to her tenant's room of course; she cleaned it, once weekly. In with the rent, she had added, proudly. Anyway, that's how she'd come to find him; today was cleaning day. There had to be some kind of foul play didn't there, since the corpse had leather straps around its wrists and ankles? If she'd known he was that kind of boy, that kind of thing going on under her own roof, she would never have allowed it. The police had begun their methodical search, but the landlady had directed them to look under the bed. She had discovered the boxes a while ago, but had said nothing to her tenant, of course. It wasn't for her to look, really, she had admitted, refusing to be embarrassed by her own nosiness. She just happened upon them while she was cleaning. She wouldn't have mentioned it at all, except, in the light of what had happened, they might be of some interest. She had thought they were just full of junk; but you never know, do you? The discovery of the human rib, to the horror of the landlady who fell uncharacteristically quiet, threw even more suspicion onto events; that and the fact that the actual tenant seemed to have vanished.

On certifying that the man in the bed was indeed dead, the doctor had commented that it was sad that such an old man had subjected himself to this kind of 'perversity', he had called it; indicating the leather bindings on the man's wrists and ankles. But he doubted the police diagnosis of heart attack; closer examination had revealed a very fine hole which had pierced the heart. The corpse had thinning white hair, and even in its' shocked expression you could see the many lines and creases that crossed his face. Liver spots dotted his hands. The wide-open eyes looked like they had seen a world of pain.

I would have loved to have seen them getting the contents of those boxes dated. Surely they would have? Even the police would have to realise they were of more worth than mere junk. Museums would be queuing up to get their hands on some of those little treasures! I can imagine the looks on their faces. Not to mention the bone; I wonder what forensics made of that? But it wouldn't take me there; it chooses the time and the place, not me. I have a box under my bed too; though mine is a large, metal, lockable trunk, but I do my own cleaning. My latest addition is a heavy, cut-throat razor…

SILENT NIGHT

The wind jangled the blank sign endlessly on its wrought iron post. The picture and wording had long since worn away, the wood within the iron frame was rotting; soft flakes of it crumbling to the frosted ground even as Sean burrowed deeper under the covers in an effort to find sleep. As if to deliberately prevent it, the sign gave a sudden, prolonged rattling as though in furious defence against the elements; like a prisoner in chains. Sean gave up; he sat upright, mindless of the chill on his bare shoulders and searched for the time. It was there, glowing neon and smug in the gloom, waiting for him; 12:52. 12:52 on Christmas Eve, Sean mused and then realised that it was not in fact Christmas Eve any longer, it was Christmas day. No kids himself and yet he was about to get up and go downstairs. Oh, the irony. There was no justice. His business partner, brother and father to his two small nephews, Mike, was doubtless sound asleep on the next floor up, curled up close to Jane; all of them oblivious to the time and the racket outside although, Sean realised, it had become much quieter now. He shrugged on his dressing gown and stepped into his tatty old slippers, unwilling to tread the cold wooden stairs barefoot. The pub was still in the early stages of redecoration. It had taken them the best part of eleven months and more money than Sean cared to calculate to modernize the pub and make it fit for public use again. That had been part of the appeal. He and Mike had been all the keener to buy the place when they learned that it had always been the site of a pub or an inn, probably further back even than the seventeenth century they had been able to trace it to. There were even rumours that it had started life long ago as a grand hall, though there had never been anything found to prove it. So, they had endeavoured to make it as authentic as possible, retaining where they could the older features of the building. Recreating history as far as the builders and the bank account would allow. The re-carpeting hadn't yet been completed and bare flagstone and wooden boards still made up most of the flooring on the ground and middle levels. Doubly grateful for his slippers, Sean flicked the brass light switch set into the wall, expecting the flame effect, sconce lighting to give off its soft, welcoming glow and illuminate his way down the stairs. Nothing happened, the landing remained stubbornly dark. Sean frowned in irritation and flicked the switch a few more times; totally dead. Yet another minor flaw in Jefferson's Electrics' supposedly reliable services.

There had been a lot of little hiccups; builders arguing about tools gone missing, kitchen fitters complaining of taps turning on by themselves. After yet another bout of cursing and head scratching, Jefferson himself had suggested the whole place needed rewiring, so erratic were the connections. He looked perplexed when he had passed the news on to Sean and Mike.

'*Unbelievable bunch of cowboys,*' Sean thought, not feeling much in the way of Christmas cheer yet, '*anything to squeeze out another penny.*' He picked his way carefully down the stairs, using a faint slant of light from the window high up in the wall to help him. Jane had wondered how they would ever manage to clean that window, as high up as it was. '*What on earth use is it there?*' she had exclaimed. Mike had joked that at least they would never have to clean it; it was so out of the way, no one would ever notice the dirt. Sean safely reached the door at the bottom of the stairs. It had a tinted window bearing the legend '*No Unauthorised Entry,*' stencilled directly onto the glass. From this side, Sean could read the phrase in reverse. He also knew that screwed into the wooden panels below it was a second notice in bold black lettering, reading, '*Beware of the Dog.*' They hadn't yet bought a dog, unable to agree on the breed, but Mike had insisted that the sign alone should be deterrent enough to any would be burglars. Sean had cause to doubt that for a fleeting moment. A shadow, fleeting but unmistakable, flitted past the tinted window. Sean's hand, cold on the door handle, hesitated. Had he imagined it? It had come and gone so fast he was left wondering if he had really seen anything at all. Convinced that he had seen *something*, he considered retreating and alerting Mike.

He mulled it over briefly then decided against it. It was horribly early on Christmas morning, still night-time really; Mike would be up soon enough as it was if the boys had anything to do with it. He would check it out for himself first; see if he couldn't handle it alone. Maybe he *was* seeing things; too much coffee and too little sleep will do that to you, he mused. Gingerly, he opened the door, feeling an irrational nervous fluttering in his stomach. It led into a passageway that bore doors left and right leading into the main bar and the lounge, as well as the toilets, the fire escape and the kitchen. It was what, he now realised, he thought of as the hub of the house. His foot scraped across the bare flagstone floor, making him jump. He grinned at himself, partly out of disbelief at his out of character jitteriness but also, he recognised, as a defensive action. His way of saying without saying, *'I know there's nothing to be afraid of.'* Feeling foolish, he let the door swing shut behind him. The corridor loomed darkly ahead, suddenly seeming far longer and colder. He flicked another light switch; again, the lights remained stubbornly dead. Determined not to give in to his growing desire to turn back, Sean fixed his sights on the kitchen door, midway down the corridor, and set out towards it. The lights crackled electrically and blossomed into life when Sean was about two paces away. He froze, finding oddly that the light was not as reassuring as it should have been. His heart was pounding in his throat, *"Bloody Jefferson!"* he swore, *"This wiring's messed up completely."* Speaking defiantly aloud. He pushed the kitchen door open and immediately a blast of frigid air left him breathless. Covering his mouth with the end of his dressing gown sleeve, Sean adjusted his breathing. Why the hell was it so cold in here? God forbid the outer door was open; then he would have to wake Mike, maybe even call the police. Maybe a freezer had been left open? The lights in here were faulty too, but at least Sean had a solution to that. Ignoring the fridges and freezers, all shut tight, hulking in dark corners like humming monoliths, he went to the range cooker. Fumbling in his pocket for his lighter, he lit all eight of the range's hobs. The sight and warmth of the flame made him feel a little better, 'God, we are all so primeval,' he laughed to himself.

He could see that the outer door was firmly shut and locked. Finding no obvious explanation for the ice-cold air in here, he resisted the impulse to light a cigarette; afraid his shaking hands would be an admittance of his unease and instead relished the heat for a while longer. The room felt eerily still; Sean discounted the possibility that some intruder was hiding within. He would have given himself away by now, or rushed Sean as he had come in; even made a break for the outer door, though the locks still in place on it would have prevented any quick escape.

He could do with a brandy; a large one. Sean turned around, preparing to push through the double swing doors into the lounge bar. He stopped in his tracks when he saw through the panes that the large Christmas tree beyond twinkled softly with pretty fairy lights. Sean's blood ran cold; his voice deserting him, rendering him unable to assert to the darkness that it was due to the electricians' incompetence again.

'How can the tree lights be on? They're not even plugged in. I checked. I always check.'

He sensed rather than felt a sudden, jerky movement beside him. The flames on the hob burned blue and low; bitter coldness descended on him like a shroud. He turned in dread of what he might see. The strange figure of a man appeared before him. He was dressed in a shabby array of garish clothing; his feet clad in pointed shoes; so much so that the toes were attached to the ankles by a length of cord stretching back over the foot. An equally ridiculous hat adorned his head, flopping down over his dark eyes in three drooping triangles, each one topped with a small bell. He held a staff, the end of which also supported three bells; they jingled gaily as he gestured to some audience that Sean could not see. His smile was rigid, fixed; more painted on than real. He appeared to be standing on solid ground, shuffling and hopping as he did, but that could not be so. There was no floor beneath his feet. He was in mid-air. Sean stood rooted to the spot, watching as the nebulous figure pranced and bowed, the horrid grin on its' mouth belying the hard look in its eyes. An overwhelming feeling of humiliation and resentment stole into Sean's conscience and he wanted nothing more than to tell him to stop, to cease his foolishness. Sean's embarrassment for the entity was nearly overwhelming, almost greater than his fear. He was mortified. Then the flames on the hob reared high and yellow again and the apparition was gone; just as silently and suddenly as it had appeared. Overcome with relief, Sean sagged to the hard floor, sobbing and gasping; alternately giving thanks for his safe deliverance, and begging God not to let it come back. He would never have believed he was a religious man. He had just enough presence of mind to turn off the gas before he abandoned the brandy and the now dark tree and hurried back to the stairs, dreading the reoccurrence of the vision each time he turned a corner. He kept expecting the jingle of bells from behind him and found himself jumping at shadows. The lights were on in the corridor, the switch still in the 'off' position. Sean barged through the door and raced up the stairs, wanting only the security of his room and his bed. He was a full-grown man in his prime, yet he craved nothing more than to hide his head under his bedclothes and urge the morning on, like an over-imaginative child. The awful thought that his room might not be safe assailed him even as he entered it. But no one awaited him there; there was no bone-jarring coldness or a heavy, eerie stillness. Just his empty room, exactly as he had left it. Sean crossed to his bed. His mind raced; already keen to deny the evidence of his own eyes. He hadn't seen it! *How could he?* It was absurd! A floating man! He could just imagine Mike's face if he was ever stupid enough to tell him. His pulse rate slowing gradually, his breathing righted itself. Even as he accepted that sleep was truly lost to him tonight, his eyes grew heavy and closed. What had he wished as the figure danced before him? That it would *cease his foolishness?* That didn't even sound like his own thoughts.

Unbelievably, he slept. As he did, the sign beyond

his window rattled so violently it almost came free of its fixings. If Sean had still been awake this would have worried him even further. The night outside had fallen still, barely a breeze on the air.

For a moment Sean felt he'd woken to just another day; bright, cold and crisp. Then he recalled that it was Christmas day. And then he remembered. He sat up sharply, braver in the daylight but keen nonetheless to get downstairs and into the presence of his family, warm and real. He dressed hurriedly and raced down the stairs. They all turned when he burst into the living room, welcoming expressions on their faces. The children rushed him, showing him this toy and that game, clamouring for his attention. He let them engulf him, grateful for their boisterousness and the excuse to stop thinking. They spent a traditional family Christmas together, exchanging gifts, eating and drinking. Sean submerged himself in it; or tried to. All day long his thoughts kept going back to the apparition in the kitchen.

The more he thought of it, the more it seemed to him a tragic figure. In the light and warmth of the living room it was easier to find some pity for it, rather than fear. Sean could not shake off the feeling of utter embarrassment he had felt on its behalf. It, *he,* had been the subject of ridicule all its' life no doubt; however long ago that may have ended. Somehow, Sean just knew that was what it had been showing to him in the depths of last night; it almost felt like a cry for help. The evening was drawing in. Sean felt a growing unease about what the night ahead might hold. All his previous concerns of becoming a laughing stock were long gone; Sean needed to speak to his brother. He waited until Jane ushered the boys up to bed, each of them insisting that they were not tired even as they rubbed their red eyes and yawned unrestrainedly. Sean watched as Mike kissed them both affectionately goodnight. He waited until they were on their noisy way upstairs before he spoke. Mike was doodling on the back of a Christmas card envelope. "Fancy a quiet one?" Sean asked, waving a can in his brother's face. Mike grinned and took it, "They wear you out don't they? The kids I mean. Don't worry mate, they wear me and Jane out too. Still, Christmas wouldn't be Christmas without them eh?"

Sean nodded smilingly. He wasn't sure where to start. He hoped his brother would keep on talking, offer up a natural break in the conversation when he could broach the subject without making a big deal about it. Mike fell quiet, seemingly content to sip his beer and share his company, still doodling idly in a preoccupied fashion. Suddenly Sean knew exactly what to say. He had been toying with the idea of telling Mike what he'd seen, even confessing his fear it would happen again, and the words had been hard to find. But now he knew just what to say and he wasted no time in saying it. "Mike, I've been thinking about the sign; you know, the name of the pub," he began.

Mike stopped doodling, "Yeah?" He asked, suddenly intent upon his brother. "Well, I've gone along with most of the things you and Jane have wanted to do here. To be honest I haven't really got a problem with any of it; but there is one thing that I want to insist on Mike, and I really mean this. It's important to me. I know it's Christmas day, and I don't want to argue or anything, but I've made my mind up on this one." "Go on," Mike encouraged, both hands still now; uncharacteristically not even attempting an argument. "Okay," Sean took a breath, "I know what we should call the pub." Mike said nothing, just glanced down at his sketch. Sean took a deep breath, *"The Jester,"* he said.

The minute he spoke the words he knew he'd done right. An inexplicable feeling of satisfaction came over him; all trace of fear and confusion, that lingering humiliation, gone. "I don't believe it!" Mike breathed. He had gone deathly pale. "What?" Sean asked, alarmed. Mike shook his head, words seemingly beyond him. He stared down at the envelope he held in his trembling hand, then leaned forward, proffering it to his brother, "I don't believe it," he repeated. Mystified, Sean took the paper.

"My God!" he murmured softly when he saw what it bore. Mike had not been doodling idly. On the white envelope he had sketched a sign. Even from this rough drawing it was obviously made of wrought iron with a wooden face. Sean recognised it instantly; it was the same sign that had kept him awake almost every night since they had moved in after the rebuilding six weeks ago. It was their sign. But there was more than that. On the wooden boarding, in fine detail, complete with floppy hat and tri-belled staff was the figure of a man. A jester. Sean looked up at his brother. He had lost his white pallor and there was a reassuring look of excited interest on his face. *"The Jester*, you say?" he repeated, a sparkle in his eye.

They had shared a few more drinks after that, in celebration. It hadn't helped; Sean had trouble sleeping again. He thought he had done the right thing in naming the pub 'The Jester.' He believed it was in some way an appeasement; an atonement for ancient wrongs. So why now could he not sleep? It took him a long time to work it out. The wind blew round the house, stirring up the trees and whistling through even the smallest of gaps, making the night sound colder than it really was. But the sign? There was no heavy, metallic jangling; no rusty, protesting creaks. No scraping. No battering. The sign rocked gently and quietly back and forth on its beam, like a baby in a crib; content. Sean smiled and drifted into peaceful sleep.

Downstairs, in the hub of the house, a faint tingling of bells frosted the air. The wall lights blossomed gently into life, the switch still in the 'off' position, as the jester, with his wide grin and eyes full of pain, bowed to his audience.

ALISSA, FALLING

"It's not winter in here you know," Alissa said, tapping her head with one finger and giving a smile of such radiance that, in another setting, might have made Jacob believe she was nothing more than serenely happy.

Yet here she was; here they all were. Atop a cliff face, frost-rimed, grassy dunes at their backs, a vast grey expanse of sky and sea before them, the roaring tide below. Raucous waves collided noisily with the rocks in an ancient battle the sea would perhaps one day win.

Jacob could only wonder at the battles raging in Alissa's mind. She stood there before him, naked head to toe, her discarded cloak at her feet, her boots lost somewhere amongst the dunes. She was still smiling, he saw, though her hand had fallen to her side once more. She appeared frail; small and vulnerable against the buffeting wind. Yet she stood calm and unmoving.

That there was something wrong with the scene before him, aside from her obvious, morbid intentions, began to play at Jacob's thoughts; now that shock had released its grip just enough to allow him to think again.

Alissa stood like a statue. Not a muscle in her delicate frame quivered in the effort to withstand the force of the wind in order to remain upright. Jacob, a good deal larger than Alissa, was fighting to stay on his feet. Alissa's skin, which should have puckered and shrunk against the stinging cold, remained as smooth as marble, as evenly pale as alabaster. It showed no sign of blotching or patching as spiteful shards of icy rain tried relentlessly to pierce her. Her hair remained perfect in her bun; tight and close, not even the prettily arranged tendrils of deliberately loose curls were moving. She did not shiver or tremble with either fear or cold it seemed. She was unmoving.

Jacob dared to dart a look past Alissa to Howard, who approached her from the other side. When they had finally spied her down at the cliff edge they had both run, recklessly, madly, to get to her. They split as they neared her, knowing instinctively that their best chances of catching her before she fell would be to take her from both sides. Howard had been silently inching forwards and was now closer to her than was Jacob. The men locked eyes for the briefest of moments, a quiet acknowledgment between them that they were each ready to make their move.

Jacob focused his gaze upon Alissa. It seemed she had not taken her eyes from him since he reached her first, only a few moments ago; an eternity ago. Was she even aware that Howard was there too?

"He won't reach me in time," Alissa stated, as if answering his thoughts, her voice as hard and flat as her eyes were bright, "He is too slow. All men are, you know; too slow."

Her eyes narrowed. Jacob felt the wind fall away at the sudden intensity of her scrutiny, as if the way she looked at him now, the way she *saw* him, was the most powerful force of all. "Except perhaps you Jacob; perhaps you are not as slow as the rest. Could it be that you are the quick one?"

The speed and grace with which she fell was almost beyond comprehension. Jacob found himself thinking her arms were more wings. She stretched them out gracefully, putting one delicate foot forward to rest briefly on a rock worn smooth with time and now slippery with ice. He saw that foot bear all her weight as she rested on it fully, lifting the other from the ground as if to take a step forward; but there was nothing to step on to. Time itself seemed to freeze as she held a pose like a ballerina in a child's music box. Then she simply dropped away.

They could do nothing but watch her fall, tossed and twisted by the wind as it finally had its way with her. Jacob could not bear to see her crash to a stop, dreading the thought of what the steely sea and spiteful rocks would do to her tender flesh. He shut his eyes tight, cursing himself for a childish coward. When he finally reopened them, he saw Howard had turned away, also unable to look. He was shaking his head in disbelief, rubbing his fingers at his temples as if worrying at a burgeoning headache, moaning softly.

Jacob had never felt so helpless or so futile in all his life. She had been wrong; he had not been the man to save her.

He could not even find words to speak. Neither could Howard, it seemed. He looked back at Jacob, his visage one of perplexity and dismay. Wordlessly, they trudged back to the horse and cart they had left waiting for them at the top of the lane; there was no rush anymore.

"She was ever troubled," Howard spoke at last. His words formed small clouds in the dim carriage; they wisped away to nothing, reminding Jacob of Alissa as she fell.

"She was," he agreed gruffly, his throat too thick to say more.

Silence fell between them. The carriage clattered over frozen clods of earth, jolting its passengers. The motion became smoother as it found the highway again, the journey less bone-jarring. Jacob tried to recall if the race to the cliffs had been as rough and supposed it must have been, given the speed they had urged the driver to put his horse to in their bid to get there in time. He could not recall it now; it was as if time had stopped with Alissa's death and he was just waiting for it to start again.

"We were too slow," Howard said wonderingly, as if to himself.

"She said all men were," Jacob added, "Except…"

"Except?"

Jacob sighed, "She said perhaps I might not be as slow as other men," he was surprised to find himself blushing at the recollection, "she was wrong of course; I was as slow as the next,"

The change in the atmosphere was so subtle Jacob thought at first he was imagining it.

"The next man being me," Howard said, his tone clipped, sharp.

Jacob cursed inwardly, "I meant nothing by it Howard, forgive me,"

"It is true though, is it not? I was the next man,"

"It was all such a long time ago,"

"Not for you. You never gave up hope of winning her back,"

"Howard, please,"

"I thought at times she still wanted you too. I saw how she would look at you, as if she was hungry for you,"

"You imagined it!" Jacob did not have the strength for this now.

"I imagined nothing!"

"Oh, what does it matter now, man? She is lost to us both!" Jacob shouted, a flash of anger rippling through him.

Howard recoiled, as much as if Jacob had struck him. Jacob was instantly sorry; he had no wish to add to his brother's hurt. His own was enough to deal with. It was true he had once loved Alissa; he had been distraught when she had left him for Howard. But he had long since stopped loving her as a man loves a woman. Outside of the relationship, free of her spell, he had been able to observe her more honestly. What he had seen was that Alissa was not all that she at first appeared; or that she was more.

In Howard he had begun to see a reflection of his former self. His brother was even more besotted than he had been; utterly blind to the way she manipulated him, determining his every move, his every word. Where Howard saw only her heavily-lidded eyes, downcast and seductive, Jacob had begun to see a sly, calculating glance. Where Howard had felt her fingers brush light and warm upon his skin, Jacob had noticed the sharpened nails, seen the thin trails of ruched skin in the wake of her touch.

Jacob recalled how he had thrilled at her last kiss, believing its ferocity to be some measure of lingering passion. He had been surprised to find, when she had gone, that his lips bled. When he looked in the mirror, his mouth was bruised, its edges tinged with black.

He had tried to warn his brother but to no avail. Howard was deaf to any criticism of Alissa. Everything Jacob said was ascribed to bitterness and jealousy. When Alissa realised Jacob was trying to warn Howard, she took steps to keep the brothers apart. Howard described her actions as defensive, protective. Jacob knew them to be malicious, but there was nothing he could say or do; Howard was lost, as he had once been himself.

It was only his love for his brother that had kept him close. Alissa had hinted many times that Jacob should sell Howard his share of the house and move on. Jacob had never outright refused; some instinct telling him to do so might be dangerous. He had simply never done it.

He observed his brother, pale and subdued in the

frigid carriage. The winter light gave him a greyish pallor. Jacob thought it must be the result of shock and grief, even as part of his mind was nagging at him that something was wrong.

Howard gave a choked half-sob. Jacob's heart went out to him. In their life before, he could have reached out to comfort his brother, embraced him even. Now the distance between them was far greater than the space between the seats. His hands remained in his lap, even as his mind prompted at him over and over to look again; look *harder...*

A flurry of hailstones rattled the windows, making Jacob jump. Howard did not even notice, or if he did he gave no sign. He was surprised to see how much the day had darkened. It seemed to him the passing scenery was wrong too; or perhaps the world was so altered. Maybe nothing would ever be right again.

Where had that thought come from? Jacob recognised it as being the kind of sweet despair he used to know when he was in love with Alissa. It was not a thought of now.

He looked back over at his brother. Howard was still and silent in his seat; there was that insistence in his own mind once more, urging him to understand.

He thought back to Alissa, naked and somehow magnificent on the cliff top. How she had shown no sign of cold or indecision; how her body had not rocked with the force of the wind. Of how she had seemed suspended in time and motion when she should have been falling...

"She was a witch," he murmured, expecting to feel ridiculous at making such a statement, though as soon as he said it he knew it to be true, "Howard, she was a witch; a true witch. She bewitched both you and me. She fooled us both!"

He looked out of the window again, his heart sinking as it dawned on him what was wrong with the scenery. They should be back in the village by now, the sound of cobbles under the wheels, the walls and doors of cottages close enough almost to touch. It was too dark, even for a winter's day. The darkness was more akin to night. It was all wrong.

The carriage lurched suddenly, causing Howard to fall from his seat. He made no attempt to stop himself, did not throw his arms forward or cry out in surprise. He fell almost into Jacob's lap, Jacob knew with sickening certainty the minute his hand touched Howard's cold flesh that his brother was dead, his mottled expression showing in the wan light through the window. Howard had not sobbed earlier; he had drawn his last breath even as Jacob had sat wondering what was amiss.

Alissa was behind this; Jacob knew it in his soul. The carriage thundered on crazily, lifting off the ground and then smashing down so hard it was a miracle it did not simply splinter and shatter, leaving him broken on the track, too.

He had to try to escape, even though he knew it was useless now. He would always be in her grip, one way or another, just as his hapless brother had been. He leaned over the stiffening corpse and pulled the handle down.

The door was wrenched from his grasp by the force of the wind. Jacob hauled himself upright, swaying madly in the rocking carriage, terrified of losing his grip to be torn and mashed by the crazily spinning wheels should he fall.

Gathering his courage, he stood as tall as he was able in the cramped doorway. For the second time that day he shut his eyes against the inevitable. Bracing himself against the door frame he took a shuddering breath, and jumped.

Two strong hands caught him whilst he was still aloft, grasping his lapels firmly and forcing him upright, holding him just above the ground as if he weighed nothing.

"Did I not say you might be quicker than most?" Alissa crowed, "No other man has ever seen me for what I truly am. A pity you tried to tell dear Howard. No matter, this way is better I think. I knew you would both come running to my rescue when you found my note. Both of you so very *dependable*," She spat the word scathingly, all pretence of sweetness gone, "Now, my love; open your eyes,"

Jacob had no choice in the matter. His eyes opened as of their own volition. Alissa was inches away from him, her once beautiful face ripped and jagged, her body shattered, limbs bent at odd angles, bruised and battered from where she had met the rocks below. A bone protruded from her upper arm, gleaming white in the too-early moonlight. Jacob was assailed by the odd thought that even her bones were beautiful.

"This way, people will find dead little Alissa and poor dead Howard washed up along the shore somewhere. They will imagine a terrible accident or a lover's tiff gone tragically wrong," As she spoke, Jacob realised that what he had thought was rain in his face was in fact specks of blood as she talked through her ruined mouth, "I can change my appearance as you change your hats. I will be a young maid, perhaps a second cousin, come to comfort you in your time of loss. No one will suspect a thing. Why would they? I will have my way after all; my man, my house, wealth and prosperity and a whole village at my disposal. And you, Jacob; you will love me more deeply and more abjectly than you ever did before. Now, look!" She forced Jacob's head around, to watch the errant carriage rumble on.

Jacob's mind was racing, trying to outthink the witch. She must have moved at speed to catch him as he fell from the carriage; did she fly? He rubbed his eyes as if they were bleary and weak, "I cannot see clearly!" he lied, "What is it you wish me to see?"

Alissa heaved a sigh and grabbed tighter at his lapels, tugging him forwards, slicing together through the chill air in a blur of dark speed to draw alongside the still hurtling carriage.

"Better?" She asked sardonically.

Jacob turned and watched, his heart pounding as he waited for the right moment. The second she released her grip even a fraction, he would act.

Jacob swore the horses galloped on thin air, prancing out over the void into nothingness. It seemed the entire vehicle and its occupants took flight before they collapsed together into oblivion.

Jacob sagged; more from terror than anything. Alissa, convinced he was beaten, loosened her hold. Jacob had to act fast.

He sliced his hands hard upward, pushing her arms wide and freeing himself of her grip. Smashing his fist as deep into her already torn face as he could, he ran, not waiting to see if the blow had felled her, dreading her hand upon him again. His fist was slick with gore and he thought madly of the slippery rock she had balanced upon before she fell.

It was only as he reached the cliff edge that he turned, gratified to see that Alissa was only just rising to her feet. There was no time for doubt or hesitation. He turned, throwing himself off the edge, as clumsy as she had been graceful, spreading his arms like wings as she had done, hoping against hope that he might fly, too.

"You were right, *bitch!*" He screamed, praying the wind would not steal his words before she could hear them, "I was the quick one after all!"

Then he fell, closing his eyes against the sight of the churning grey waters waiting to devour him, sharp rocks ready to slice at his flesh and feed him to the sea.

Alissa screamed; a gut churning screech that could freeze blood in its veins. Above, the skies boiled, mirroring the sea below. The day became darker still, matching the blackness of her mood.

"No matter," she cackled, staggering on shattered limbs towards a row of cottages in the distance, giving themselves away by lamplight, "tomorrow the village will have its newcomer; a young woman, destitute, beautiful, fragile; a woman in need of a bed and a meal in return for some honest work."

Even as she disappeared into the blackness, muttering

and cursing wetly, her hair began coiling itself into a neat, pretty bun, her skin became as smooth as marble, as pale as alabaster. By the time she reached the first cottage in the row, there was no trace of the witch to be seen; just a helpless young woman, pale in the moonlight, whose nails were just a mite overlong, if you looked close enough.

CRAWL

Hector lay in his bed, stiff with fear, straining to listen. A regular ticking sound was slowly travelling the perimeter of the room. Neon green numbers on his digital bedside clock showed him it was 4:06 a.m. He whimpered like a child and drew the covers up to his chin, clutching the sheets tightly with trembling hands.

The more Hector listened, the less it sounded like ticking. It began to remind him of fingers tapping in impatience; slender, capable fingers with horribly sharp nails…

He stopped that train of thought, afraid of where it might lead him. He tried to look at things logically. He was a grown man for God's sake. Lying in bed sweating and trembling like a frightened child at a noise in the night was ridiculous.

Hector resolved to act. He would sit up and click the lamp on, knowing the spread of light into the room would go a long way to making him feel better. Then he would cross to the wall and switch on the main light, banishing the shadows once and for all. Once that was done he would be better able to think properly. There had to be a real reason for the sound that had woken him in the early hours every morning for over a week now. To put it down unquestioningly to something supernatural was both childish and superstitious. What was it they said? The simplest and most likely of explanations is usually the *actual* explanation.

Occam's razor; that was it.

The sudden image of a razor flashed into his mind. Wickedly sharp, in his mind's eye, it was opened in a rough L-shape, blood dripping from its edge and down its handle. What bothered him most was not the gore but the fact that although the razor was being held up against a black backdrop, there was no visible hand holding it.

Hector wasn't sure if the image would be made better or worse if he could see the hand that had wielded the vicious blade.

'There I go again, letting my imagination run away with me,' Hector forced himself to speak aloud; his voice was small and he was terrified some disembodied voice might answer from the blackness.

His resolve to switch on the lamp wavered. Why was it so dark in here anyway? There should be signs of dawn creeping into the room by now, the solid blackness giving way to lighter shades of grey at least. Instead the darkness had a presence about it, as if was more than the mere absence of light. He remembered what his mother used to say to him when, as a nervous child, he protested at having the lights out at bed time, "There's nothing there in the dark that isn't there when the light is on."

It was meant to be reassuring, but it always left Hector pondering the question; what if something *was* there in the light, it just couldn't be seen? What if the dark held revelations all of its own?

No longer keen to reach out across the space between his bed and the bedside table, he instead shrunk deeper under the covers, keeping his bare arms hidden beneath them.

There was a pause in the ticking. Hector had the odd sensation that whatever was making the noise was listening now, too. Somehow the silence was worse than the sound. He almost sobbed with relief when it began again, regular and measured on its path; coming closer.

He didn't dare close his eyes, even though he could barely see anyway. Close to tears and unable to think clearly, Hector needed the light on more than ever, but he did not have the courage to flick the switch. There was definitely something in here with him. Some primeval instinct buried deep within him told him so.

Mother had told him to always obey his instincts; a contradiction to the phrase she used when turning the lights out. It had always confused him as a child, He was confused now. His instincts were screaming at him to get up and run; they were also telling him that the minute he rose from the bed and set foot on the floor, he would be caught.

The chimney breast rose upwards through the floor from the living room below. Hector was used to the kinks and knocks it made as it cooled during the night. The whole house groaned and creaked in its beams and boards; those sounds Hector was accustomed to. This new noise was a stranger. Uninvited and unwelcome, at first Hector had succeeded in dismissing it as his imagination, nothing more. It took him a while to realise that the more he tried to ignore them, the more insistent they had become. In the end he had no choice but to acknowledge them as real.

Things had not got any better as a result.

Hector focused his gaze on the solid, familiar shape of the chimney breast. The ticking had just traversed across its width; at least as far as Hector could tell. There came a new sound now; a single knock from within the chimney, so faint that if Hector had not already been listening intently he might have missed it.

He flinched, eyes wide in expectation and dread. There came a second knock, harder this time, followed by a firm rapping as if someone was demanding entry.

Hector froze, terrified of giving himself away to whatever it was. Deep down he knew the thought was a foolish one; it already knew he was there.

From beneath the flimsy defence of his bedclothes, Hector couldn't tear his eyes away from the area of the chimney breast, though there was nothing to see there and the knocking had ceased. The ticking had too, he realised.

He could not keep his body from trembling, his muscles tense and aching. He had pulled the bedsheet taut across the bridge of his nose, his eyes peering out above it almost comically. His hands were now so slick with sweat that it was soaking into the cloth, loosening his grip, the sheet losing its tension and sagging to touch his mouth. Something about the closeness of the damp cotton and his warm breath upon it served to heighten his fear. He gave a small, panicked moan and twisted his hands in the fabric, tightening it again and raising it from his skin.

He wished he had found the nerve to switch on the lamp. Now he did not even have the courage to turn his head and look at it, scared of lowering his guard in any way. The room had fallen too still.

Hector wondered how long he could lie there, trying not to move nor breathe. Tears began to prick at his dry eyes; he was helpless to stem them, some long-dormant instinct telling him he was right to be afraid. Something fundamental, something *elemental,* was out of balance here.

Eventually he had to exhale or suffocate. He let his breath go unwillingly, as if he might never get it back; stuttering it out as silently as he was able. He had become too aware of the rhythm of his own breathing and it seemed to throw it out of joint, resulting in half-breaths and mistimed exhalations; leaving him gasping like a drowning man.

The room had finally begun to lighten a little, shapes looming out of the dark, becoming more definite. When he had come to bed they had been ordinary, innocuous things. Now they had taken on a more sinister form, as if he could not trust them to be as they were when he had first turned out the light. Had his mother lied to him as a child? He would never know; not now.

Hector couldn't bear it a moment longer. He closed his eyes tight against the room, squeezing hot tears out to roll across his cheek and leave freshly damp spots on his already sweat-soaked pillow.

The ticking resumed, as did the knocking, in time together now; *tick-knock, tick-knock, tick-knock,* circling the room as if someone was behind the walls, no *inside* the walls, seeking his attention. It demanded he open his eyes again.

Hector made an unintelligible garble from the bed. Meant to be a cry for help, it came out as a strangled sound that stuck in his throat. He could not open his eyes any more than he could utter a word. The *tick-knock* had reached the wall his headboard leaned against. Soon it would be behind him. Unless he found the strength of will from somewhere to move, to get out, then he would be at its mercy.

He began to sob beneath his covers, all pretence of maturity and rationale forsaken. Occam's razor be damned. The most obvious answer was not always the real one. This wasn't an infestation of beetles or an old house wakening, nor was it a product of a fevered imagination.

Another image blossomed in his mind. On the same black background as the razor had been, a quill pen was writing words in a vivid white. Hector watched in his mind's eye until he was able to read them; *Then what am I?*

His eyes snapped open. *How do you escape what is there in your own mind, scribed on the inside of your own eyelids?* Just now he had been too afraid to look upon the room any longer; now he was too scared to see inside his own thoughts.

He could still see the words hanging in the air, taunting him. His gaze drifted inexorably back to the chimney breast. The words trailed along, hanging suspended against the chimney backdrop for a second before they faded away to nothing. The *tick-knock* was almost directly behind him now. He could do nothing to halt it, nor could he turn to face it. Even if his body had complied with his command to move, his attention was caught by something new.

The base of the chimney breast appeared to be moving. It was at first very subtle, nothing more than a shift of muted light across its base. As Hector looked on, the movement expanded until it seemed the entire base of the wall was rippling to and fro. Hector blinked, hoping the action would clear his vision.

Instead the movement changed, stretching up the height of the chimney breast; a run of channels spreading outward like veins in a bony hand. They pulsed and twitched and for a horrifying moment Hector imagined an enormous fist breaking free of the wall and reaching out to grasp him. Perhaps the hand that had held the razor…

The wall fell flat and innocent, but Hector knew it was not over. When the movement began again seconds later, as he had known it would, it had taken on a new form.

This time, it appeared as a small ball spinning slowly like a globe, beneath the sheen of gloss paint on the bricks. It travelled upward as it spun, losing its uniformity and becoming something more akin to amoeba; morphing into irregular shapes, bulging outwards here and there.

Hector's tears dried on his face as he watched, helpless. The movement had reached the point where the chimney breast disappeared into the attic floor above. Unless the thing behind the wall could move up there too, there was nowhere else for it to go.

At the top of the wall, the paint began to split and peel. It fell to the floor silently, like dead skin. Hector's heart raced, knowing that the thing that had been watching him all these weeks, marking time, was about to show itself to him.

He did not want to see it.

There was a loud crack, as if something far more solid than paint had just broken. Hector lay transfixed, unable to tear his eyes away.

Something pale and nebulous oozed out of the crack. It seemed to hover for a heartbeat, before falling horribly suddenly, the entire length of the chimney breast. It glided at speed to rise up again at the foot of Hector's bed where it rested for a split second before drifting up the length of his body, drawing level with his face just as Hector drew the sheet up entirely over his head. Hector pinned the thin cotton down as hard as he could; his only means of defence.

He shut his eyes tight and began a fervent prayer; he hadn't uttered a word to any God since he was a child. Now he was prepared to make any promise, to perform any duty, if he could just be delivered of this evil.

For it was evil. It stank of it; filling his nostrils with the strange, wet odour of fungi and rotting vegetation. There was something else in there too. Something heavy and metallic, that Hector did not try too hard to identify.

He could feel its oppressive weight, even though it was not physically upon him. He was thankful for that much at least, though he dreaded feeling its' touch. He knew its' weight would be cold and crushing, too much for him to bear.

It could see him through the sheet, of that he had no doubt. If he were to open his eyes, he could see it too.

He kept his eyes tightly shut and fell silent, his prayers and tears drying up. There was nothing to be done but wait it out and hope it let him be.

Its stare burned into him, leaving him cold. All he could hear was the rush of blood pounding in his ears and his own ragged breathing. His arms began to tire and he grew terrified of the thought that he might lower them and allow the thing to lie upon him. He was afraid his will would snap and he would open his eyes and see what it was that held him trapped in the one place that should have been a haven to him.

Hector lay there for an age. He began to despair, wondering what his chances might be if he attempted to throw the thing aside along with his sheet and dive for the lamp. Surely the light would extinguish whatever it was? Surely a thing like this belonged to the dark?

Would it be so easily thrown aside? Would it let him get that far?

He had almost reached the point where he had to try or else die in his own bed when he felt the weight lift suddenly. He knew without even looking that it had gone. Not simply moved from its position over him, but altogether gone. Even from beneath his covers the room had a lightness that was nothing to do with depth of vision. It felt cleaner somehow; purer.

Hector kept the sheet raised above him a while longer even though his arms were tired and he was exhausted with fear. He would wait a bit, be sure it had really gone, before he dared to come out from his hiding place.

Forever passed. Finally, Hector ventured to lower the sheet. The early-morning air felt cool, fresh and entirely natural upon his skin, a welcome relief after being stifled by the bedclothes for so long.

He glanced warily across at the chimney breast. There was no sign of any movement there, the paint was whole again, not cracked or flaking, Nothing hung in the air, waiting to swoop down upon him.

The whole room felt calm, a peaceful stillness rather than the foreboding silence of earlier. Whatever it was had gone for now, he felt sure of it. He would not spend another night in this place. He would devote today to making sure of that. Filled with a sudden sense of purpose, Hector couldn't wait to get out of there.

He wondered how long he had been lying in fear. It must be close to daybreak. The gloom hadn't yet lifted much, but he could do something about that now.

Hector sat shakily upright in his bed and stretched out to the lamp switch and salvation. It was as he clicked it on that the *tick-knock* began again in the wall directly behind him.

There was no pool of bright light to offer hope in the dark; no warm, comforting glow to keep night at bay. The bulb remained stubbornly dead and cold, no matter how urgently Hector stabbed at the switch.

Panicked, he swung his feet round to the floor in his need to bring the thing to life. If anything, the darkness seemed to deepen around him. The only thing that offered any sort of illumination was the neon green numbers on his digital clock. He almost laughed at the absurdity of it; the time showed 4:08 a.m.

Two minutes.

Two minutes had passed; the eternity that Hector had just endured.

When the thing came down again, silent and deadly as an owl, the last thought he had before he lost all reason was how strange it is, that time crawls when you are in torment.

Then he gave himself over to the dark.

Then nothing.

BLANK SCREEN

Dennis felt his face glowing red, physical proof of his anger and embarrassment, even though he was alone. The screen jumped before him as another member posted a message.

blueboots: Well said 2hot2handle!

2hot2handle: Thanx boots. About time someone told that pervert I think.

Dennis was furious. These gutless idiots wouldn't speak to him like that if they were face to face, without the protection of anonymity. Posting brave words onto a mindless screen was one thing. Saying it to his face would be quite another.

He posted a reply with his username. It made him feel powerful, like anything could happen when he was around. Anything.

BlankScreen: Fuck you.

He sat back, watching the monitor for a reaction.

He was not to be disappointed. There came a flurry of responses from blueboots and 2hot2handle and others. Satisfied that he had offended so many with such a simple, unoriginal phrase, Dennis folded his hands behind his head and grinned. His anger was still there, hale and hearty, but he was in a familiar situation now; fighting his corner. He felt focused.

He allowed himself to ponder on 2hot2handle a moment. Was she, he wondered, or was she merely acting out some kind of fantasy on the World Wide Web? And that blueboots. If they both turned out to be porn stars, viewers' wives or something, not real porn stars, he wouldn't have been surprised. Why had they got so touchy at his suggestive comments? They hadn't left the discussion, had they? They hadn't reported him?

No, because they wanted it really; they enjoyed it. All women did, they were just too shy or repressed or something to allow themselves to admit to it. But that was ok. Dennis knew. BlankScreen knew. He understood.

A new name appeared on the screen, one Dennis hadn't seen before.

RedMan: What's your problem pal?

He knew the question was being asked of him. Fleetingly, Dennis experienced the strangest of sensations, as if he could hear RedMan speaking those words, could see him, unshaven, hot-breathed and muscly before him, in his face. Ready. Aggressive. Dennis' grin faded. He sat upright, fingers poised over the keyboard, searching for a reply that would reassert his dominance in this uptight little chat room.

He wished it was a real room that he could stride into, pushing people aside as he did so, making his presence truly felt. He could envisage it now; see the reluctant admiration and fear of the onlookers as he leaned in on RedMan and softly said; 'You, pal. You're my problem.' He felt sure that would be enough to get rid of him in reality. That was the great thing about the net; you could be whoever and however you wanted. Most of these guys were just playing at being tough. If you pushed hard enough they'd all back off. Not Dennis though. He was tough for real. He'd see this RedMan off, double-time.

RedMan: That's right: I am your problem.

Dennis was a little taken aback. He hadn't realised he had actually typed the words. They had gone now, lost in the wedge of chat that was taking place on the thread. He could probably scroll back up and find it, but why waste time? This guy was just afraid to lose face, that's all. The screen jumped again:

blueboots: You're the problem BlankScreen. Get a life!

Dennis ignored her; stupid little scrubber trying to get in on a man's conversation. He was caught up in his exchange with RedMan. He wanted to say something clever about being the solution, about solving his problems good and proper.

BlankScreen: Fuck you too, RedMan.'

White-space silence. A computing eternity. Dennis' watch ticked away a minute. He was beginning to feel comfortable again. Then two messages appeared simultaneously.

2hot2handle: Who's RedMan

RedMan: Would you like that, Dennis?

Dennis felt the thrill of something unfamiliar race up his spine. He stared at the words, his angry mind confused, trying to identify the cause of his fear. Was it RedMan's insinuation that he, Dennis, would like to fuck a man? Somewhere deep in his subconscious a thought was screaming to be heard. *'Has he touched some sore point with that question? Am I some sort of homo?'* Dennis' anger increased. He typed what he thought was another clever response.

BlankScreen: Shouldn't you be called PinkGirl?

Which was followed by;

2hot2handle: Who? Me?

blueboots: Ignore him, he's obviously a nutter.

RedMan: Would you like me better if I was?

Dennis blushed angrily. He hit the Caps Lock key, screaming the words as he typed them:

BlankScreen: YOU FUCKING HOMO!

When RedMan replied, Dennis just knew that he was calm and cool, not in the least upset by this exchange.

RedMan: Sapiens? Or Sexual?

blueboots: Who's a homo? We are FEMALE BlankScreen. Appropriate name by the way. Couldn't get much blanker.

2hot2handle: STOP SHOUTING BLANKSCREEN!

Dennis felt absurdly, inexplicably close to tears. Who the hell did these people think they were? What right did they have to call him a nutter? Ok, so maybe they didn't like some of the stuff he'd been saying. Maybe he was in the wrong sort of chat room, like blueboots had told him.

But that was the whole point! If he'd gone into a porn chat room his suggestive comments and lewd remarks would have been unnoticed; a drop in the ocean. No one would have been shocked or offended, that's for sure. And that was the point! That's why he did this; to prompt a shocked reaction. To hear and feel their anger and indignation. There was nothing that did it for Dennis like trapping some innocent in a dialogue she couldn't get out of. The ones who were too young, too inexperienced, too shy to tell him where to go. The ones that tried to remain polite. Or pissing people off to the extent that he felt like he was the only one in there making a difference. RedMan was spoiling all that. He read the screen again. Someone had made a lame entrance to the room, saying *'Hi all! How are you?'* Dennis scrolled up, re-reading his conversation with RedMan.

RedMan: Sapiens? Or sexual?

Clever bugger. Dennis took to the keyboard.

BlankScreen: SEXUAL! It looked pathetic, there on the screen. He tried again.

BlankScreen: I MEANT SEXUAL, U TOSSER!

Almost immediately 2hot2Handle responded, obviously confused by his latest contribution to the chat. No response from RedMan.

Dennis had had enough. He shoved the power button on the hard drive with such force that it tilted backward and threatened to crash to the floor. There was an electric 'pop' as the screen went dead, then nothing. Dennis was panting as if out of breath, sweating hard.

"Bastards!" He said to the empty room, *"Bastards!"*

Who the hell was this RedMan anyway? It was his fault. He had provoked him.

'Would you like that, Dennis?'

Dennis stopped dead. The beads of sweat on his back turned cold. RedMan had called him Dennis.

Not BlankScreen.

Dennis...

THE ORCHARD

bbey relished coming to stay here. She reflected upon how she loved everything about the Old Rectory, even as ramshackle and in need of repair as it had become. She loved the rough red-brick exterior, the worn old oak door and lintel. Inside, she loved the intricately carved wooden mantles and the ever-present scent of smoke in the air, even in summer time. She cherished the view from her room; the wide, gentle slope of the neatly bordered grass lawn leading down to the dovecote. Just beyond it, over the stile, was the thing she adored most of all about this place; the orchard.

All through her childhood she had thought of the orchard as her own, claiming it through her grandparents. Although they explained to her many times that it was merely a remnant of a much larger orchard that had once existed there, that it did not really belong to anyone anymore as far as they knew, it made no difference to Abbey. The stile linking it to the garden seemed to her evidence enough that it belonged to the rectory. Confident in this assertion, she had spent many a day exploring it; picking apples, damsons and pears which her grandmother later turned into tarts or jams, or which they would simply enjoy fresh from the tree.

Occasionally she was interrupted by village children; an affront Abbey always took personally. She wondered at their daring to come here. When they appeared, shouting noisily at distance, darting through the trees screaming and laughing, she would gather up her basket and hurry to the stile. They must have glimpsed her climbing over it; in fact, she thought she heard one of them call out to her once. It was a wonder none of them had ever had the nerve to follow her over it and into the garden.

For now, it was a pleasure to wake once more in her little attic bedroom in the Rectory. Grandfather had been in to light the small fire so early in the morning that it had still been dark. Now, as the sun rose weakly in a pale sky, it crackled comfortingly, its glow warm and somehow reassuring. It had been too late when she had arrived last night to do little more than eat supper before bed. What a pleasure, to have the prospect of a whole day in front of her to do with as she pleased.

She lay in bed, revelling in the gentle glow of the fire, listening to the ancient beams of the house creak as it too awoke; moaning softly as if complaining mildly of aching bones and great old age.

Sixteen years old; a young woman now, Grandmother

had said when she greeted her at the door, fussing over how much she had grown since the summer. Yet Abbey didn't feel very grown up when she was here, she realised; here she felt like a little girl again, full of all the excitement of a child about to rediscover a much-loved pleasure.

The familiar view across the garden to the dovecote was unchanged, except this morning it was becoming dotted with flakes of tentative snow. It hadn't begun to come down in earnest yet, but the skies were full and heavy looking and an air of gentle anticipation hung over the whole house. Snowing on Christmas Eve!

Abbey tried not to let her excitement show, though inside she hoped fervently that she would wake to a thick blanket of snow on Christmas Day. She dressed hurriedly and went downstairs to tell her grandmother that she was going out for a walk.

"Let me guess where to!" Her grandmother smiled, "I told your grandfather we wouldn't be able to keep you out of there for long! Don't you want some breakfast first? You'll need something inside you to keep you warm,"

"I'll have it when I come back, I'll enjoy it more then," She kissed her grandmother on the cheek and pulled the latch on the back door, "I won't be long, you stay in the warm," she smiled, closing the door behind her.

Outside, Abbey was surprised at just how much snow had already begun to settle. There was very little green left exposed on the lawn; the roof of the dovecote was already covered. She shivered, shrinking deeper into her coat, pulling her hood up and shoving her gloved hands into her pockets.

It was sufficiently deep to leave footprints as she walked. She brushed the snow off the top beam of the stile and swung her leg over, her foot slipping slightly and causing her to lose her balance. She squealed and then laughed out loud, the sound muted in the cold air. She dropped easily down into the orchard, feeling immediately at home.

It was as if the place knew she was there. There was an intangible sense of adjustment to the air; a change of atmosphere, as if it was acknowledging her presence. Abbey felt a sudden rush of affection; she stroked the trunk of a nearby tree in response. The tree shivered, sending down a shower of fresh snow, making Abbey laugh again.

She wandered aimlessly into the depths of the orchard, mindless of passing time. There was no fruit to pick this time of year. She had left her basket behind, intent only on enjoying the orchard for itself. She regretted it when she came upon a holly tree, its prickly leaves resplendent in a shade of glossy, deep green, juicy red berries dotted here and there like candles on the Christmas tree. She stepped off the path and removed a glove to stroke one of its smooth, thick leaves; perhaps she would come back later and cut some for the dinner table.

She yelped in surprise and pain as she pricked herself on the sharp tip of the leaf; a tiny red droplet of blood formed on the end of her finger, in imitation of the berries. She put her finger to her mouth and sucked, turning back to the path.

She was shocked to see how heavy the snowfall had become in the few moments she had been distracted. It fell like a thick curtain before her eyes, settling on her lashes, making her blink hard. The wind had grown too; a low howl slinking through the orchard as if a pack of ghostly wolves were on the hunt.

Abbey shivered. She was warm enough inside her coat, but the air had become heavy with something more than snow.

In her peripheral vision, a shape flitted between the trees. Startled, she flicked her hood back for a clearer view. Surely none of the village children would venture out here this early in the day, in weather such as this? It must be her imagination; or else the falling snow making shapes, tricking her eyes.

There it was again; a shadow a shade deeper than any other. A shape too solid to be snowfall, too nebulous to be properly seen, but there nonetheless, she was sure of it.

She watched as it darted in and out amongst the trees, not pausing for more than a second before flitting like nervy deer to hide amongst the undergrowth. There was more than one; the shapes tall, like her; peering out from behind the cover of the tree trunks or from under the shelter of a bush.

For the first time in Abbey's memory, she was suddenly afraid of the orchard. Convinced the shapes were watching her as much as she was watching them, she sunk her foot into the deep snow on the path in her haste to get away. The snow came up and beyond the top of her boots, to sink cold and wet against her stockinged legs.

The wolf-wind gave a howl. The sound of laughter came from deep amongst the trees. Abbey gathered up her skirts and mindless of the drifting snow, ran.

She had never seen snowfall like it. Her grandfather had told her of harsh country winters when he was a boy, but she wondered if even he had ever witnessed it like this. It was already more than halfway up the stile. If she had left it much longer she might not have been able to discern it at all. She fell more than climbed over it, the pattern and shape of the garden utterly lost now, all things buried in mounds of glistening white. It would have been quite beautiful if not for the cold fear in Abbey's heart.

She was struggling back to her feet, breathless, when there came the sound of a deep splintering and snapping. Abbey stopped in her tracks, straining to listen. Could that have been the trees, groaning beneath the weight of the snow? She didn't dare look for fear of what may have followed her.

It came again, more protracted this time; a strained, unearthly protestation followed by a grating, sliding noise. Abbey tried to run up the gentle slope of the lawn but she was impeded by the depth of the snow. She fell more than once; by the time she reached the top she was covered head to foot in sparkling crystals. She paused for breath. The grating sound came again, followed by soft, heavy thuds. It seemed to be coming from the front of the house.

Using the rough brick wall for support, Abbey forged a path round the front. As she rounded the corner there came another solid thump. She jumped back in alarm; one of the cumbersome slate tiles from the roof had missed her by inches.

Horrified, she watched as several more followed. She looked up, her heart sinking as she finally understood what the terrible groaning noise had been. The roof of her beloved Rectory had begun to give way under the enormous burden of the snow. It sagged perilously in the middle, pipes and beams sticking up and pointing skywards accusingly.

Another groan, this one deeper and more foreboding than any she had so far heard. It galvanised Abbey to move, and fast. Her grandparents needed warning; they had to get out of the house.

The snow had already begun filling in her footsteps. She half-ran half-slipped, screaming for her grandparents, but they did not seem to hear her.

Her throat was raw with shouting and the frozen air by the time she barged into the kitchen, sending the door flying. Her grandmother was not there. Breakfast had long since been cleared away; there was no sign of her or of grandfather. They could be anywhere in the house, tending to chores as they always did; polishing the old wood, making the beds as if there was nothing wrong.

Skidding perilously on the tiled hallway floor, Abbey scrambled to the foot of the stairs, all the while calling; her screams becoming choked with sobs, her haste slowed by panic. It took an age to climb the stairs. When she finally reached the top there was no sign of them anywhere on the first floor. Could they not hear the death throes of their poor, dying old house? Couldn't they hear it falling apart?

As Abbey reached the stairs leading to the attic rooms there was a deafening roar. The whole house quaked, bringing her to her knees. The floorboards began to ripple, the pictures on the walls slipping to hold weird angles, the spindles on the stair rail bending and snapping. The carpet runner rolled like an errant wave.

Her grandmother appeared at the top of the staircase, rigid with fright, her face pale as moonlight. Grandfather stood behind her, his face set, determined, hands on his wife's shoulders as if urging her forward. Abbey motioned to them with her hand; *we must get out, we must get out now!*

Abbey watched helplessly as pure white snowflakes began to fall around them, absurdly prettily as the roof opened above her grandparents' heads. They made an odd cameo for the briefest of moments, Abbey staring up at the two of them as her grandfather wrapped his arms protectively about her grandmother and gave Abbey a profoundly sad smile.

Then the old house heaved one last, gasping breath and the world came splintering down around them.

"So I need to tell everyone you're too scared to come?"

Denny glared at his older brother, "I just don't want to go Mike, that's all. It's Christmas Eve! There's loads of good stuff on the telly, loads of nice things to eat downstairs…"

"Everything on the telly is either rubbish or a repeat we've seen a thousand times already, and Aunty Pat and Uncle Glyn won't be here until tea time, so that's no excuse is it? We've got all day if we want it,"

"I'm not spending the whole day in the orchard Mike,

are you off your rocker? It's freezing out; it's going to snow they reckon."

"Nah, they always say that. Everyone knows it never snows on Christmas Eve, except maybe in kids stories,"

"It snowed on one Christmas Eve though didn't it?"

Michael grinned, "So you are coming then? I knew you would…"

Denny sighed, "No I'm not coming! Look, I know you don't believe me, but I really did see the Orchard Ghost, okay? I don't want to see her again."

Michael pulled a face, "Why not? What did you say she looked like?"

Denny shrugged, "I've told you before!" He sighed, relenting, "A bit older than us, long dark hair under a hood. She was wearing an old-fashioned coat; you know, long, like a dress, with a cape on it. She turned and looked at me Mike; she looked right at me,"

"Doesn't sound too scary to me Denny, I must say,"

Denny clearly remembered the encounter he had last Christmas, "It was a cold day; not frosty or anything, just a bit cold. Damp, if anything. But she was covered in snow, top to toe. It glistened all over her, like someone had sprinkled her with glitter, or she'd rolled in it or something. How could that be Mike?"

Michael's voice dropped to a whisper, "Did you see her face? How did she look at you?"

Denny thought about the stories he'd heard all his life about the ghost, famous in the area. In those stories her face was always bruised and misshapen, supposedly hit by fallen beams, or bloodied, blackened and torn where the fire had taken hold; or else just frozen in a twisted scream of horror. Denny had seen none of that; only the simple, open face of a young girl, her expression one of abject fear, "She looked like any other girl really Mike; except she looked scared to me,"

"Scared? It was you who had seen a ghost!" Michael laughed.

Denny half-laughed in return, "Yeah. But you know what Mike, when I say she looked at me, I mean more than that."

"You do? What do you mean?"

"I mean, well I don't know; I don't believe she just happened to look in my direction, or just by chance glanced my way. She looked right at me Mike; really *looked* at me. She *saw* me,"

Michael shoved his hands in his pockets and examined his younger brother closely. He looked like he was telling the truth. Besides, it wasn't like Denny to shy away from an adventure or two; he still looked pretty frightened.

"But why would she be scared?"

Denny shrugged, "Maybe she thought she was the one seeing a ghost?"

Mike's brow furrowed. He tried to make sense of what Denny had suggested. "You mean, she was the one spooked by you?"

"Maybe. Look, I've thought about this a lot and I think," he paused, "promise you won't laugh?"

"I promise," Mike assured him, his face serious.

"Okay. Well I think that when I saw her, it was before it happened to her, you know? Like she was caught in the time before the house collapsed and killed them all. I think she saw *me* as a ghost, someone out of time and place for her, and that's what scared her,"

"But what about all those other stories, when people see her battered or burned?"

"They must have seen her *after* it happened," Mike pulled a doubtful face, "Look I don't know Mike okay? I'm not saying I have all the answers, it's just what I've been able to work out; that's all. It's the only thing that makes any sense to me,"

Mike shivered, "Poor girl," he said, surprising Denny with his unusually thoughtful remark, "I wonder what it must feel like, to be caught in time like that; reliving something that awful over and over again?"

As if in answer there came the sudden, insistent pattering of wet snow flakes against the window, like fingers tapping on the pane, beckoning them to come closer.

Denny and Michael shared a look. The tapping became more insistent, snow forming a small pile on the sill to begin building its way up the pane. Together, they crossed to the window; Michael opened it as wide as it would go, sweeping the freshly gathered snow aside. They both looked outside.

"I think maybe I'll stay in after all," Mike muttered, the chill air creeping into the room and making his words drift away on small clouds of vapour.

Outside, the trees and hedgerows, already rimed with a hard, glittering frost, had begun to bear the weight of the heavily falling snow. Even as they watched, the lines of the pavement, the kerb an9d the road out front began to blur and merge into one. They looked up; behind the screen of snowfall they could see the sky was a leaden grey, full of so much more to come.

Normally clearly visible, now they could barely make out the form of the ruins of the Old Rectory and the remnants of the orchard. The snow was falling so hard it was all but blinding. As Denny pulled the window closed again the wind began to gust the snow into small drifts.

Across the village, from the grounds of the orchard, came a long, low howl; as of wolves, come a-hunting.

THE FACE OF
THE GALE

Andy's skin was raw with the wind. It tore into him as if it meant to rip the flesh from his bones. When he had come out barely twenty minutes ago it had been nothing more than mildly chilly, so he had thrown on his usual leather jacket. Now he was beginning to wish he had chosen something warmer.

He dug his hands deeper into his pockets and bowed his bare head against the elements. Shards of rain had entered into the fray, hitting him with spiteful, stinging blows. For the briefest of moments he considered turning back, but it was not really an option; he had a date to keep.

He turned right onto the high street, hoping to find it more sheltered than the back roads. He was disappointed; if anything, the wind picked up its pace here, though now it was at his back, pushing him. Rather than hastening him on, it made him clumsy; stumbling over his own feet, tripping on uneven paving slabs as they seemed to rise up to meet him.

Cursing, Andy pulled his hands free of his pockets, holding his arms out for balance. It crossed his mind that he must look ridiculous, like some ungainly, flightless bird. Then he realised the street was empty; no one was around to see.

"I must be the only idiot stupid enough to come out in this," he muttered.

As if in answer, the wind gave a sudden shriek, shrill and piercing. Wincing, Andy clapped his hands over his ears. The sound was all pervading, his hands affording him no defence against it whatsoever.

Hunched, Andy stepped off a broken kerb to cross an alley way. The moment he lost the protective shelter of the shop fronts he was exposed to a vicious sidelong draught. It punched into him, hard and deliberate, driving the breath from his lungs and making him double over.

He gasped, staggering to a wall for support. He couldn't believe the violent turn in the weather. It had felt like a real blow, like a fist slamming into him and he began to wonder if he should turn back. Who else would be likely to turn up to the meeting in these conditions? He fumbled in his pocket for his phone, checking for a missed call or a text to say it had been cancelled.

His fingers were numb with cold as he tried to negotiate the keys, frustration bubbling in him as first they and then the phone refused to do as he asked of them. When he finally got them to comply, the screen showed him neither a new message nor an unheeded call. It glowed with the network logo, gave an irritating beep and went dead, its screen black and useless.

When the hell had the wind ever felt like a real fist hammering into his ribs?

He didn't allow the question to fully form inside his mind, though he was well aware that it lurked there. It unsettled him; that seed of understanding that something was wrong. Denial was far more comfortable, was something he was used to. Everything was fine; everyone knew the weather could be unpredictable, even dangerous. Later, when he was safely home nursing a coffee in front of the T.V he would laugh at the absurdity of it.

For now, his heart felt anything but light. The weather had a heavy, repressive feel to it and he wanted nothing more than to escape it and take shelter somewhere. The small centre they met at was still a few streets away. Decision time; carry on the path he was set on, or turn back?

'Your choice Andy; up to you.'

He pushed away from the wall, bracing himself for another buffeting. "Okay, you win; I'm going home," he said aloud, turning on his heel and preparing for a battle as he took the gale head on.

The wind dropped so suddenly that he stumbled forward, its invisible presence not taking his weight as he had expected it to. Andy stretched out his hands to take the impact of his fall, his wrists taking the brunt of it and sending thrills of pain up his forearms. His knees were grazed beneath his jeans. He could feel the hot sting of scraped skin. A small patch of blood bloomed on one knee, staining the denim darkly.

The street fell eerily quiet. Andy realised it was not just the roar of the wind that was abruptly absent but all the racket it caused; debris clattering up the road, bins shifting, shutters rattling, anonymous metallic clanking high up amongst the cables and gutters. Everything was utterly still.

Andy shifted onto his backside, rubbing his knees. He looked around the street for someone to share his embarrassment and disbelief with. He had just been physically assaulted and floored by the wind. Now the day was utterly calm and peaceful, as if he had imagined it all.

He stood shakily, gazing about stupidly, confused as to his next move. It might be best to go on. At the centre he could at least rely on tea and sympathy.

He shuffled about, looking from one end of the street to the other, mentally calculating his options. It would take him maybe another ten minutes to get to the meeting, about the same to get home. At least at the centre there would be others to talk to. A group who would no doubt also express their astonishment and disbelief at the elements; a group he could be a part of. At home he would be alone, talking to himself as usual.

He decided to go on. He would try to pick up the pace and get there a little quicker, just in case the weather turned again.

Decision made, he turned and walked on. He kept his aching hands and sore wrists free of his pockets, in case he needed them again, though he doubted how well they would hold up to a second fall.

A growing sense of being watched began to assail him. There was no sign of life on the street, not even a bird on the telephone wire or a cat on a sill. Perhaps there was someone lurking behind one of the panes of frosted glass…

A small dread knotted itself in the pit of Andy's stomach. He tried not to notice even as his mind showed it to him; all of the windows on the street had become laced with frost. Every shop window, office front, windscreen and wing mirror bore a film of crystalizing ice. He saw too, that his breath had become visible on the air, issuing from him in small clouds of steam.

The feeling that someone was watching his every move intensified. Andy fought off the urge to run, somehow knowing that to do so would be a mistake. He forced himself to keep to a brisk walk, though his eyes were everywhere. The sense of impending attack was almost overwhelming.

He slowed his pace as he drew alongside a Jeep parked at the kerb side. Like all of the other cars on the street, its glass was frosted over, but some movement across its hood caught his eye.

Andy came to a complete standstill and watched, amazed. The ice on the windscreen seemed to creep outwards from a centre point like something living, sending tendrils like raised veins to spread across the body of the vehicle. It trailed across the roof and doors, small off-shoots forming and growing; reaching out as if searching for something, reminding Andy of the spreading arms of some voracious jungle plant.

He watched, fascinated, as the ice journeyed on, webbing across the wheels until their circular shape was completely hidden; stretching out frozen tips towards the pavement.

He stepped back hurriedly out of its reach, its enchantment broken. Now he saw the whole of the street behind him was encased in ice. It heaved and cracked as it travelled, popping and groaning as if something below it was trying to break free. It was coming his way; coming for him.

Andy dropped all pretence of calm and ran. Not yet forty he wasn't an old man by anyone's standards, but the sudden exertion taxed him. Adrenalin got him past the first two hundred yards, but the years of self-neglect and devotion to vodka soon caught up with him. By the time he reached the end of the street he was gasping for breath, his ribs ached and he swore the stitch in his side would kill him if the ice didn't get to him first.

No sooner had he regained his breath than his joints began to scream at him, his knees and ankles inflamed and afire. He could do no more than give them a cursory rub; he could feel the cold reach his back and knew the ice had caught him up.

He tried to fight off panic, looking around for somewhere that might afford him refuge. He saw the bus stop across the road, as yet untouched by the elements and standing, innocent and normal, waiting.

"Screw this," he panted, "I'm getting a bus home, this weather's unnatural,"

He crossed to the stop, his need to sit down and ease

the pressure in his knees overwhelming. His relief when he sat down on the cold, unforgiving metal bench was tremendous. The sharp spasms had reduced to a dull, constant throb. He closed his eyes, unable for now to focus on anything other than his pain.

It took some time for Andy to realise that the popping and cracking, the straining creaks and groans, had stopped. He opened his eyes. The ice had reached the end of the road and begun to spread like white ivy over the walls of the buildings there. It had almost reached the eaves, fanning out prettily across the bricks, when it had frozen still, as if caught in the act.

The silence that fell was heavier and more oppressive than the quiet that had followed the sudden drop in wind. The atmosphere was one of foreboding; the air full of something more to come. Andy shifted uncomfortably on the cold, hard seat and leaned forward, glancing skywards through the bus stop's clear roof.

Clouds raced across a deepening sky, forming strange, fleeting shapes. One moment they billowed so densely it looked for all the world as if they could be touched, if only you could reach so high. The next, they were thin and wispy, feathering out, twisting, coiling and forming again; mesmerising.

Andy looked on as they changed form yet again; towering like tidal waves, so tall and threatening he recoiled in dread. A second, darker wave slipped in beneath, rolling out flat and wide. Andy shuddered, grateful beyond measure that they were not waves, after all.

There was a sound not unlike the constant, steady roar

of the ocean. It reached his ears from some distance away. Andy tore his eyes from the roiling skies and looked about him, checking that the ice had really halted its advance and was not seeking him out once more.

That was what was wrong, he suddenly understood. It was not simply the freakish weather that was so disturbing. It was the way in which it seemed to be responding to his presence; as if it was *personal*.

The ocean-noise continued from afar. A low, steady rumble of something ancient and unstoppable; something lulling, calming and deadly…

"Get a grip man," Andy said, though his voice rang false and hollow in his own ears. He stood painfully and checked the as yet un-vandalised timetable in a plastic display window, then checked his watch; there should have been a bus by now.

He knew in his heart there would be no bus today. Not a single car had passed him by, not another living soul had crossed his path since he had stepped out of his front door.

He would not be riding home in safety in comfort and he could not even begin to contemplate walking back down the ice-laden street he had just escaped. His body was too full of pain and too weary to consider going the longer way round. Even if he did choose that path, who knew what might be waiting for him as he walked?

He resigned himself to the fact that he really had no choice but to go on to the centre. He hoped there would be someone there, despite the emptiness of the streets.

He thought briefly about knocking one of the anonymous front doors; but what would he say? Who would be likely to admit a strange man with an even stranger tale to tell when he rapped upon their door? That's if anyone even answered to his knocking in the first place. He looked at the row of cold, hard houses and knew without even trying that it would be a waste of time.

The centre it was then; the sooner the better.

Andy was about to leave the meagre shelter of the bus stop when a thought came to him.

He had first experienced the wrath of the wind when he decided to carry on to his original destination. The second time, when the ice had made an appearance and as good as chased him down the road, he had once more talked himself into carrying on until he reached the shelter.

He had just made that same decision to go on for a third time. What would the elements inflict upon him next as a result?

He stood in stunned realisation, his mouth agape, his expression one of moronic vacancy even as his mind raced, trying to make sense of it.

It couldn't be the case. This was the vodka talking; or rather, the result of long absence from it. His mind was playing tricks on him, trying to scare him out of going to the support group that had played such a major part in getting him this far. He had been dry for months now. Some part of his psyche must be rebelling; testing his will to kick the habit for real.

The thought that some elemental being was trying to deter him from the meeting, was trying to *punish* him for it, was nonsensical in the extreme.

He gave an odd, humourless laugh. What would the others

say when he told them about this particular hallucination? Some of them had shared some humdingers up to now, that was for sure; but this had to beat them all hands down.

Andy hadn't experienced much by way of hallucination; more drunken misunderstandings and occasional flights of fantasy, akin to vivid daydreaming or the 'flying elephant' variety of imagining. To have as good as convinced himself that the weather was out to get him was something else altogether.

He looked up sharply, all at once afraid that there was no advancing ice sheet layering the street opposite. He felt a rush of absurd gratitude when he saw that it was indeed there, clinging cold and harsh to everything in its path. He hadn't imagined it; that was something.

He rubbed his side where the wind had punched him, holding his jacket aside and pulling up his shirt to expose a roughly circular bruise in shades of blue and purple over the spot where he had been hit.

He looked in terror up at the skies, at once certain that those tidal clouds were about to come smashing down upon his head, sweeping him away, bashing him apart, flooding his lungs and drowning him in fathoms of cold, choking air.

Instead the sky had become less towering, if still heavily grey. The huge billowing clouds were gone, replaced by twists and swirls that moved so fast they barely held any shape or form for more than a moment.

Andy released his breath in relief. Perhaps if he hurried, perhaps if he directed his thoughts elsewhere, he might get to safety untouched.

He took a tentative step out of the shelter, expecting some momentous crack of thunder or bolt of lightning to strike him down. Nothing happened. Encouraged, he stepped back out onto the street.

Keeping a wary eye on the ice, he began to make his way. The wind did not resume, the ice did not move, the clouds stayed where they were. By the time he reached the next corner he had begun to think that it had been his imagination after all. Perhaps it was the effect of alcohol on his mind; God only knew he had abused it hard enough for such a long time. A man couldn't treat his own body with that much disdain without suffering some sort of consequence for it.

The burning pain in his joints had eased to a warm, dull ache, though his gait was stiff and awkward. There was a time he would have hit the bottle to find relief. Now he craved nothing more than a hot bath and a hot drink. He smiled inwardly, finally relaxing a little. He had experienced some freak weather conditions, that's all; global warming had a lot to answer for.

He was tired, his vision becoming blurry. Head down, watching his own footfall, Andy rubbed at his eyes as he walked, blinking rapidly as he tried to clear them. It took a minute for him to understand that the problem wasn't with his eyesight at all.

The pavement was slowly disappearing from view. Every step he took, each one slower than the last, his feet became more deeply enshrouded in a layer of mist. It swirled and danced, ebbing and flowing at his movements; looping and coiling as if it meant to trip him up. It began to rise, thickening as it went; climbing his ankles, his jeans, reaching his groin like rising smoke.

Andy felt sick with fear, this time acknowledging that his dread was justified. This was not some awesome freak of nature. This was something else entirely, and it was meant for him.

He wanted to sink to his knees, weak with fear, but to do so would allow the mist to consume him. He reached out for something to grasp; a railing, a fence, anything solid and real. His bare fingers brushed against something wet and spongy. It made him think of fungi growing in dark places and he drew his hand back sharply, holding it to his chest, subconsciously covering his heart.

He heard a sigh in his ear. It was a harsh, wintery sound, drawn out and chilling. Andy shuddered, trying to get his bearings. The centre couldn't be too far off now; if he could just keep going.

The mist was making his clothing heavy with moisture, each step increasingly harder to take. It rose to shoulder height, forcing Andy to walk on tip-toe in a bid to keep his head above it. He stumbled on a step or two, terrified of falling again, but it was futile; moments later the dry-ice mist had engulfed him completely. His vision reduced to zero, Andy had no choice but to stop.

The wisps of cold cloud began to solidify before him. Ever swirling and eddying, the shape it was making never held for long, but it was unmistakable for that. Now Andy did fall to his knees, his frozen hands still clutched to his chest as if to prevent his heart from escaping it.

A huge head hung in the mist. It was there, then it was not; wind-tossed and warping. The face was disc-like; round and flat with vast, empty eyes and a wide, gaping mouth. Its edges frayed and tore with the wind that pulled at it, ribbons of mist curling outward to disappear into the frozen air.

Impossible to believe that eyes that were nothing more than holes in the fog gazed upon him, yet they did; of that, Andy was absolutely certain. They filled him with a solid, cold dread the like of which he had never before known.

The gaping mouth puckered, the cheeks became pinched and convex. Andy became aware of a rushing sound, as of air being drawn inward. Paralysed with fear and fascination, he realised what the sound was; the giant face, whatever it was, was breathing in…

He knew what was coming, just as he knew there was nothing he could do to stop it. He opened his mouth to scream but that action served only to allow the blast of Arctic breath greater access to his warm insides.

Cold needle shards tore at his tongue and his inner cheeks, finely shredding his lips, ruining his throat as they raced towards his innermost core. His eyes, his whole face, were ravaged by the silvery splinters. It was relentless; tiny, elemental arrows slicing into his body at speed upon the eerie exhalation. It turned his hair into a frozen mane, frosting him to the pavement, colder and stiffer than rigor mortis, freezing his last thought in its tracks.

He had looked into the face of the gale and was forever lost.

When life returned to the street it was slow and sluggish, its occupants vaguely aware of being somehow out of time. The pervading feeling of suspended animation lingered a while, though no one quite had the presence of mind to remark upon it.

The weather was, as it always is, a topic on many people's lips. More so since the discovery of a body on the pavement; just sitting there bold as brass, an unwelcome reminder of just how fleeting life can be. They were saying he had died of hypothermia, though there were some rumours that he had also been an alcoholic. Popular opinion seemed to suggest that it was a mixture of the two factors that had caused the poor man's death.

The newspaper had reported that the pictures of the man's corpse were too graphic to publish, though they hinted at a face torn to ribbons and blue with cold. An expert gave a quote that the condition of the corpse was similar to those of errant novice mountaineers who hadn't taken the climb seriously enough. He protested surprise at finding such extreme effects in the middle of a small town, but no one appeared to be taking him seriously.

Andy's lifeless body was loaded into an ambulance. It took off, sirens wailing unnecessarily. Police followed them away; no sirens blaring, just a silent blue light flashing in a circular motion on the car roof.

Danny Hackett, four doors down from all the commotion, reasoned he had seen all there was to see. He turned to climb his front steps, needing the support of the metal hand rail to get up them.

He pulled his hand away abruptly, the stinging cold

pain from its touch causing him to gasp. It didn't feel that cold outside…

He rubbed his palm and looked down at his hand, dismayed to see a fine web of blue veins covering it, spreading up his wrist and lower arm.

Rattled, the old man climbed the steps slowly, without the aid of the rail. He would put the kettle on, have a hot drink, maybe put a blanket over his knees while he sat and drank it. That would sort him out.

He shut the door. As he shuffled into his kitchen, flicking on the light in the rapidly darkening day, he never noticed his breath becoming visible on the air, nor the thin layer of ice that crusted the front door window and lined the edges of its frame, sealing him in…

The following is an excerpt from *Hay's Breath – A Collection of Witchcraft and Wickedness* by S P Oldham, released as an e-book in October 2016.

PROLOGUE

O nce Upon a Time…
        There Once Was…
        A Long Time Ago, in a Far Away Land…
That is how fairy tales are meant to begin. They tell of magical creatures in haunted forests; of ill-treated maidens locked in tall towers. Of frail humans made to face inhuman tasks. They tell of an evil that is always ugly and of a virtue that is always beautiful. They share the joy and relief of the inevitable Happy Ending for the deserving, and they recount the dreadful fate endured by countless wizards, gnomes, goblins, elves and above all, witches.

To children, these tales are terrifying yet compelling, horrible yet exciting. The adult mind faces a similar contradiction in that it, too, loses itself in the evil-doings of the woman-in-the-woods, whilst at the same time always knowing that there's no such thing as witches…

THE SISTERS: SUSSURATA

The forest sleeps.

Another quaint phrase from the old fairy tales. Evocative perhaps, yet untrue.

The forest does not sleep. It is not even quiet or still, if you listen closely. Twigs snap, leaves rustle; claws scurry, scratch, scrabble and rake amongst the foliage and dirt. Creatures moan, snuffle, yip, snort, bark and croak. The forest is always wide-awake and full of life; and life, for the most part, is noisy.

There is another sound. It reverberates like an overlay upon the general hubbub. It is there and it is not there all at once; a non-sound that is only missed when it stops.

Sussurata wanders the forest at night. Tall and stately, her elegant form drifts amongst the trees, blending with the shadows. Her long grey hair hangs down her back like a lustrous, silky cloak. Her face and neck are as smooth as any young maiden's, and as pale and waxen as the moon. Her sensuous lips bear a subtly serene smile; her green eyes glitter with humour, as if she is enjoying a private joke only she understands.

Her dress is exquisite. A fitted velvet bodice adorned with a pattern of creeping ivy hugs her slender waist, lifts her delicate bosom. A skirt falls in pleats to her feet, gently brushing against her immaculate soft-skin boots; all in shades of grey to match her hair. The skirt would seem to human eyes to be made of satin, or something like it. It falls like satin, is cool to the touch like satin; it catches the eye, like satin.

It is not satin; nor is it merely a skirt.

The garment is what gives the witch her name. Its soft susurration as she drifts through the forest is the sound that overlays all the other noises of the night. It whispers beguilingly with every step she takes. Even when she is motionless, the skirt murmurs on, feathering the air with its litany.

Sussurata's house, because of course she *must* have a house in the woods, is hard to find. The forest does not merely grow right up to its borders, but grows all over and around it too; taking it into its earthy embrace. It is so thickly entwined with mosses and lichen, grasses, boughs and branches that at first glance it appears to be nothing more than a particularly dense patch of thicket. Only the most observant, those most willing to deny the instinct to turn and run, notice that there are windows and a door, even a chimney stack amongst the tangle.

Sussurata leaves it every night to roam the forest. She travels to its outer edges, collecting items for the pot; sometimes for stews, sometimes for potions. She looks out across the horizon, keeping a weather eye for her sisters, Sibilanta and Silhouetta.

She hunts.

She returned to her hidden home after one such night roaming the woods, small creatures skittering hurriedly away at her footfall, to find all was not as she had left it.

A patch of scorched earth marred the ground in front of the door. Ragged, burnt holes in the walls were repairing themselves even as she approached.

Sussurata strode forward, her door swinging open before her, welcoming her home. It closed softly behind her as myriad candles blossomed into light and a hearty fire sprung up in the grate. She poured a goblet of something hot to drink and sat down.

"I see you have been up to your tricks again," she took a sip.

"Did you expect anything less?" a voice rasped in reply.

Sussurata smiled. She wrapped her hands about the goblet as if to warm herself against its contents, "I expected better. Your attempts at escape are the most feeble I have ever known,"

"I am perhaps older than any you have ever caught before,"

"Is great old age not desirable in a witch? Should you

not be endowed with such vast power and wisdom that you are too formidable an opponent for me?"

"I was, once. Now I am so old that I have forgotten more than even you will ever know,"

Sussurata smirked, "Yet I knew enough to capture you,"

The witch in the cage suspended above her head fell silent; thinking, cursing her own stupidity.

Frail Agnes had known, of *course* she had known, of Sussurata's reputation. But she had believed herself too wily and too learned to ever fall prey to her. True, Agnes had not gone out of her way to cross the witch's path when she ventured into the woods; nor had she worried overmuch about meeting her, should they chance upon one another.

That had been her first mistake.

Agnes decided to try a different approach; one of antagonising her captor. It was a dangerous ploy, one which could so easily backfire, but she hoped to enrage her enough to make her distracted. If Sussurata should lose her cool composure for even one moment and do something reckless or unplanned it could prove useful to Agnes. All her hopes hung upon the witch's arrogance and vanity.

"Great old age also teaches us reverence," she said, "We choose our victims carefully, with deliberation. We know which step is a step too far and we endeavour to avoid making it. Your mother would never have shown such disrespect,"

The silence that fell was immediate and palpable. It

was a long time before Sussurata spoke, tight-lipped and sharp, "You will not mention that hag again,"

It was a command that brooked no room for further discussion. Agnes groaned inwardly; another mistake. Sussurata may be vain but she was no fool; she had not lost control as Agnes had hoped. She suspected that all she had succeeded in doing was making her angry and in a witch like Sussurata, anger is a cold, hard thing indeed.

Frail Agnes let some time pass before she dared to speak again. She chose her words carefully this time, allowing a note of admiration into her voice, hoping she might be able to flatter where she had failed to provoke.

"What is it you intend to do with a prize such as me?"

Hag's Breath – A Collection of Witchcraft and Wickedness
by S P Oldham

Official website of S P Oldham – So Lost in Words:
http://solostinwords.doodlekit.com/

S P Oldham on Facebook:
https://www.facebook.com/solostinwords/

S P Oldham on twitter:
https://twitter.com/dogskidssmiles

S P Oldham on Goodreads:
https://www.goodreads.com/author/
show/15116823.S_P_Oldham